# Apalachicola Pearl

D1636718

## Michael Kinnett

Published by:
Southern Yellow Pine (SYP) Publishing
4351 Natural Bridge Rd.
Tallahassee, FL 32305

www.syppublishing.com

This is a work of fiction. Names, characters, places, and events that occur either are the products of the author's imagination or are used fictitiously. Any resemblance to actual persons, places, or events is purely coincidental.

The contents and opinions expressed in this book do not necessarily reflect the views and opinions of Southern Yellow Pine Publishing, nor does the mention of brands or trade names constitute endorsement.

ISBN-10: 1-940869-78-1
ISBN-13: 978-1-940869-78-0
ISBN-13: ePub 978-1-940869-79-7
ISBN-13: Adobe eBook 978-1-940869-80-3
Library of Congress Control Number: 2016948651

Printed in the United States of America
First Edition
August 2016

# Dedication

To the unrecognized author & poet that is my mother,
Marilyn Jean Kinnett

# Acknowledgements

The city of Apalachicola, Florida, and the wonderful people who cherish and preserve its history.

The Orman family, for archive materials.

Special thanks to friend and Editor Sue Cronkite for her hard work and insights.

# Preface

War is never noble, and the motives for war are never pure. Men of politics, commerce, and religion driven by the great evils of the world, such as greed and envy, mask the reasons for war, wrapping them in a flag of nobility. Uneducated sons of the poor, good and decent men of the South, stepped up and answered the call to form a new country, a Confederate States of America. The new government would be better able to represent the agricultural economy and could keep southern dollars in the South. It was not long before these gallant young men defined the Confederate cause as, 'a rich man's war but a poor man's fight.' The real reason for the war became painfully clear with the Emancipation Proclamation in 1863. The poor Confederate soldier was now fighting for the Southern aristocracy's right to own slaves. The Florida Panhandle between Marianna and Apalachicola became filled with deserters as the noble Southern cause turned to dust.

I have trouble comprehending how some men lack conscience. In the War of Southern Independence, these ruffians plundered and pillaged wherever they went. Under the guise of patriotism, they preyed upon citizens who remained behind. In my story, I will introduce you to one of these groups in the form of the Rebel Guard. I hope you will gain the overwhelming spirit and determination of the people who stayed in Apalachicola. Those remaining not only had to deal with the Union blockade but also the battle from within against the ruffians and their own Confederate government.

My sincere wish is that you will enjoy reading about Pearl as much as I enjoyed writing about her.

Please remember as you read, the records of history seldom reflect the trials of the people living through the events.

The telling of this story begins in the present-day with the discovery of two journals I found hidden beneath a floorboard in the attic of the Orman House Museum. I have completed the first journal and present it to you now under the title, "Apalachicola Pearl." The following are the writings of Michael Brandon Kohler.


Michael Kinnett

# Introduction

# Michael Brandon Kohler

It is July 4, 1886, my sixty-fourth year in this delta town. I was born in 1822, just one house over at the old home place on what would become the corner of Columbus and Laurel. Now an old man, I sit once again awake, unable to sleep, reviewing my journal, one that should encompass my life. But with age comes wisdom, and I now see that the history we write is like the river that flows through my town; it has great power but always seeks the easy path. As I review my own words, I see the lies that embellish and feel once again the emotions omitted.

History written by men reveals no cowards except those of the enemy, tells of great deeds of worth and cause, but shows only one face, and fails to distinguish the testimony of those consumed by its passing. We sit like gods on the pinnacle of our lies, convinced of our own omnipotence, and too late we realize it is through truth we will find enlightenment. Many will seek the grace of God, but few will find it. I grow tired of my own lies and now wish only to be one of the few. "And ye shall know the truth, and the truth shall make you free," John 8:32. Perhaps, somewhere in the words I will find peace, and some young man might avoid my curses.

Looking back, I find it hard to imagine how a little Pearl could become my greatest treasure, define my life, and give me purpose.

# Chapter I

## Living the Path We Choose

July 4, 1859: I am thirty-seven years old today. Please God, let me sleep. At times, the heat and damp of summer take me to the limits of my reason. I lie for hours, simmering in a mattress of wet cotton with the smell of my own sweat, the stench of the low tide, and the never-ending hum of the mosquitoes. In my mind, I could justify loading a ball and primer and believe God should forgive those who do.

One o'clock in the morning, five more hours before the blessed sun will rise, and maybe then, I will find hope once again.

Yellow Jack is paying a deadly visit. Two months ago, nearly four thousand finished the cotton-shipping season; now in July, we are seventy. Of those who stayed behind, thirty-four became infected with Yellow Fever. Of those thirty-four, there were five survivors. Yesterday, until dark, I helped to dig graves, and now I find myself alone and tormented, lost in the dim light of my room with paper and pen.

My thoughts are many and scattered. I cannot make sense of all the talk coming off the ships. Deep inside, a fear is growing. Great changes are coming; I know not good or bad. Even in the nature of this place, something is wrong—wrong with the air itself. The Apalachicola River is different, slower, and more shallow. Prosperity is waning, and dark attitudes prevail. The light hearts and visions of the 1830s and 1840s have all but disappeared, replaced with an ominous revelation, a future of uncertainty, and a feeling of foreboding.

Why did I stay behind? Family in Boston wrote, inviting me to visit during the fall season and looked forward to my arrival, but I was the first generation born in the South, and I felt it was my responsibility to remain here.

In 1822, President James Monroe appointed a port collector for the newly completed Customs House at the Port of Apalachicola. From the settlement known as Cottonton, a city came into existence and was named Westpoint.

It was here, in this small town at the mouth of the Apalachicola River, that my father Brandon Michael Kohler had accepted the position of customs agent. He and my mother, then two months with child, sailed into the port of Apalachicola, Florida, arriving in Westpoint in January. On July 4 of that year, I, Michael Brandon Kohler, was born. Here, the Kohler family began a new chapter in our family history—a Southern history.

My father felt the move South was good and believed we stood witness to the beginning of a new and prosperous port town. My mother knew that the cold winters of the north had never suited him and that he spoke often of warmer climates.

My mother used to tell me stories, from before I was born, of my father and the prosperity he found working in Boston as a young man. A customs cutter at the port, he recorded the comings and goings of ships and the collections of monies and tariffs. It was due to his connections that later I was afforded the privilege of attending the Boston Latin School.

In Boston, I boarded with my mother's brother. My uncle, William James Harris and his family, lived just blocks away from my school. I vividly remember the brisk walk to the south side of School Street where the impressive Boston Latin sat, peering down, judging me as I entered her doors. I sometimes laughed aloud when I looked at myself in the mirror, thinking how Hatch and Jacob would disapprove of the dress code there and me having to wear shoes. I missed the feel of the sand between my toes.

In letters from home my father expounded on how proud he was and how the Customs House hadn't run smoothly since my departure. In my mother's letters, although I could not see her, I could feel her crying. The pain of separation was almost more than I could bear.

Owing to my early schooling at the prestigious Boston Latin, at fourteen, I passed the entrance examination to Amherst College, starting as a sophomore. Since I would not be going into the clergy, two years was all that was required for my diploma. At the age of sixteen, when school ended, I looked forward to returning home.

Strange are the memories that follow us. Education came easy to me, so I have no nightmares about lessons or study. What I do remember from my time at Amherst were the many nights I found myself freezing in the upstairs room of the dilapidated boarding house. I soon understood my father's aversion to the snow and ice of the Boston winters. I often thought of the warmer southern climates of home and missed the company of my parents and friends.

I loved my father very much and cherished days I spent working at his side, helping at the Customs House. Some days I worked in his stead when he was under the weather. I was proud when people called me young Mr. Brandon or Master Brandon. In my youth, the only people who called me Michael were my mother, father, and best friends Hatch and Jacob.

In 1839, when I was seventeen, my father invested in his own business, Kohler Ship Chandler and Mercantile. He and my mother moved twenty miles west to the city of St. Joseph. I stayed behind in Apalachicola, and with my father's spotless reputation and his recommendation, I assumed his position at the Customs House. The job paid well enough that I could live comfortably. My mother was saddened to leave me behind and felt no comfort when Hatch and Jacob offered to keep an eye on me.

"Who's going to keep an eye on you two?" she responded.

I understood why my father wanted to move, not only for a better opportunity but because St. Joseph of the 1830s was a beautiful city. Some referred to it as the "Queen City of the South." St. Joseph was a rival port, and businessmen there tried to steal our cotton trade; some citizens of Apalachicola called it the wickedest city in the country, referring to it as the "Sin City of Florida." Its large, brick-fronted hotels were called brothels, and the beautiful women of the town were said to be ladies of the evening. The brandy they drank brought on drunkenness, and the town, according to some, became a pit of debauchery.

Cotton season ended in June of 1840. Locals began to leave, fearing the seasonal heat might generate the swamp gases believed to carry the Yellow Fever. There were reports of sickness, but a few of us stayed. As expected, the heat of July and August was repressive and relentless, but to our surprise, there was to be no fall or winter, and the heat pushed through to November. The five months to follow brought rain and seemed more like spring. Some who had left learned of the fair weather and returned early.

In 1841, I was nineteen, had a Boston education, and was living and working in Apalachicola. This new and growing port city prospered in the footprint of the former Westpoint. Incorporated in 1831, Apalachicola now shared the name of the river it served.

My family in Boston found it amusing that I lived in three different towns—Cottonton, Westpoint, and Apalachicola—but never moved more than a few city blocks.

In May of forty-one, an unnatural heat and damp fell upon us. The fever gases lying dormant in the swamp returned with a vengeance.

My friend Hatch knocked on my door early one morning. Deathly pale and noticeably disturbed, he asked me to follow him downtown. As we walked, he explained that a preacher from St. Joseph posted a list at the city hall.

"Michael, it's bad. St. Joseph's been hit hard by the fever."

"What's the list, I asked."

"It's a list of the dead."

My body trembled as I made my way through the crowd gathered around the list. There were no fewer than a dozen pages hanging from the wall. I began combing through the names. My heart sank as I realized each page carried four columns of names, and the print was very small. I scanned the list for what seemed like an eternity. Suddenly I stood paralyzed with my finger pointing to my parents, Kohler, Brandon/Cora.

Forty-one was a hard year up and down the coastline. Of the people who remained in Apalachicola, one hundred perished at the hands of

Yellow Jack. So many died in St. Joseph that pits were dug and bodies piled on one another to place them underground as soon as possible. Within the months of May and June, seventy-five percent of the city of St. Joseph fell to the Yellow Fever.

Contrary to the advice of many, I rented a mule and headed for St. Joseph. I rode hard, pushing the poor creature to the brink of death.

It was no surprise to see Dr. John Gorrie at the hospital, assisting the sick. Dr. Alvan Chapman stayed behind in Apalachicola, but because of the sheer number of sick and dying in St. Joseph, the two friends realized the greater need and felt obliged to assist.

Dr. Gorrie's skill and compassion were unequaled, and his documented studies of the Yellow Fever made him the ideal candidate.

When Dr. Gorrie saw me, he approached and hugged me. He knew, and it was as though his own parents had been the victims.

He told me the bodies of my parents were recovered from my father's sailing skiff which was out in the bay. My father had evidently rowed my mother offshore, in hopes that by breathing the fresh air of the Gulf breeze contagion might be avoided. In haste, Dr. Gorrie drew a quick map of where he believed their bodies were taken and the pit in which they were laid. He then took a handkerchief and rolled mint leaves into one side.

"Take this Michael, and tie it around your nose and mouth. Keep the mint near your nose. It will help keep you from vomiting at the stench.

"One more thing Michael. I hesitate telling you this, but you will probably discover it for yourself. Please keep in mind your father was in the advanced stages of the fever. He had the black vomit and would have died anyway had he not been shot."

"Shot," I cried out. "What are you talking about?"

"Chances are some looters came across your father's skiff and hastened his death to rob him. I am so sorry to be the one to tell you," said Gorrie.

"What about my mother?" I asked.

"I can assure you; she had already died of the fever," Gorrie said.

I turned and ran as fast as my legs would carry me toward the cemetery.

Following Gorrie's map, I found the pit and began to dig through it for the bodies. Wakes of buzzards and a murder of crows circled like dark clouds and filled the trees. Harvesters of death perched on oak limbs, biding their time.

"Damn you black devils," I screamed.

Slaves stood with shovels of dirt to cover the bodies.

I threatened them. They were attempting to layer the dead, covering each row of victims with soil before more were placed on top.

"I'm looking for my parents. Hold your shovels," I cried.

I searched three hours, shifting bodies, stiff like pine boards in rigor mortis, before I recovered his body.

I held him in my arms and cried, trying not to look at the grotesque shapes of the dead around me.

I continued searching for my mother well into the night, lighting a lantern, refusing to give up my search.

I was thankful Gorrie had given me the handkerchief. The mint helped with the overwhelming stench, and the hankie kept me from breathing in tens of thousands of mosquitoes. I fared better than the other searchers who had soaked their handkerchiefs in a garlic solution or camphor; they seemed to gag and vomit more frequently.

As I worked, smoke from the fires surrounding the pits helped to disperse the horrid little insects. The buzzing of mosquitoes and flies sounded like saws slicing timber.

The smell of the burning sulfur pots was horrendous. I never viewed the burning of sulfur as an effective deterrent or curative for the fever.

Then, on the far end of the pit, I noticed a fabric sticking up between two bodies. Beneath the bodies, I found my mother. I cannot believe I felt joy standing in this pit of festering corpses. If not for the dress she made herself, I would not have recognized the face of my own mother. It had been a few days, and the atmosphere of this place fueled the process of decay. Carrion flies laid their maggots in the flesh of the dead, and it looked as though the flesh moved. Getting my parents out of this pit was the most dreadful task I ever performed.

Dr. Gorrie, having arrived earlier with others, had no means of transport back to Apalachicola, so I left him with my mule. Gently wrapping my parents in blankets, I loaded them into my father's sailing skiff and sailed for home.

I brought them back to Apalachicola, laying them to rest in the Chestnut Cemetery near a large magnolia, my mother's favorite tree. The Vicar's ceremony was short, as he had many funerals to officiate during this terrible time.

Articles of the time, appearing in the *Pensacola Gazette,* posthumously recorded the dark event.

> "Daily showers filled the noisome marshes surrounding the city with lukewarm, fuming water; the moist, hot air was sweltering and in marsh and swamp, as well as from the numerous ditches that interlaced the city, so many messengers of Death...to be stricken was to die.
>
> Secretly, silently, this fateful guest stalked through the busy streets, stole into store and offices, tete-a-teted with the beauty and chivalry of the city, and charming entertainments touched hands with the many who wined and dined in the public hostelries and frolicked with old and young in this memorable year of 1841.
>
> One morn, the news flew throughout the city that there had been a death from Yellow Fever. Bankers ceased counting money and discounting bills, lawyers laid aside their briefs and turned their thoughts to this unconquered enemy of mankind, doctors pored over their books and papers seeking for the then unobtainable knowledge wherewith to combat successfully the mortal disease, the newspaper stopped its press that it might insert the news, merchants quit offering their wares wondering what the outcome might be, while mothers clasped closer their offspring thinking thereby to shield them from impending danger.

Other days passed, and more deaths were announced. Processions to the burying grounds beyond the Cypress swamp at the rear of the city became frequent. The powers of the Negro gravediggers were taxed to the utmost to open sufficient graves for the oft-recurring processions. The limited stock of coffins was exhausted. The high Carnival of Death had opened most auspiciously. It had already eclipsed and ended all festivities. Cheeks that were but the day before flushed with youth and beauty now blanched with fear.

Uncontrollable fear seized upon all. Business ceased. Ships slipped their anchors and stole away into the night. The air was stagnant and filled with pestilential vapors. Many sought safety through flight only to be stricken and die by the wayside. Soon the horrid pestilence held undisputed sway throughout the city. Deaths were no longer counted. All day long was heard the rumble of the death-wagons upon the streets. Trenches took the place of graves and rude boxes of coffins. Half crazed, men would rush to the surrounding woods for safety with heads bursting with inexpressible pain and eyes forcing themselves from their sockets. Under some lofty pine, they would check their mad flight, hesitate, stagger, then the dark blood, the black vomit of death, would come rushing through their parched lips. They would fall forward into this pool of deadened blood—and die."

"The heretofore prosperous city was doomed. The death angel held undisputed sway. As he passed from door to door, he found no blood-stained lintel as in the days of yore. Few were spared. Families were broken up by flight—only to be soon reunited in death. How quickly love, hatred, the passion for wealth, for learning, were placed in one common receptacle! How insignificant was man. Reason, humanity, charity, all had fled. Like the dumb brute of the woods or field, man died uncared for and alone. In a very brief space of time, the city was depopulated.

The few who were spared, remained for a while to dispose of the property, often left without living beneficiaries. The famed city of St. Joseph was dead."

Every town has its darker side, and I was in the worst of ours when I walked into Blood's Tavern after the burial. This was a place where the lowest rung of men gathered, those made of labor and sweat. The regulars were transients who once a year drifted into town to find work in warehouses or who unloaded cargo, like salt, from the bowels of ships. They then moved to the next port, trying to stay one step ahead of what was to become their fate. It was a place rarely frequented by upstanding local citizens.

I sat at a small table nursing a strong, unrecognizable drink. Whale oil lamps tried, but failed, to cut through the smoke that hung thick like a fog. A warm breeze made its way around the buildings but offered no relief. Instead, it drifted through the alley where it picked up the foul stench of urine and vomit.

In my mind, I recited the words the Vicar spoke at the graveside, trying to find comfort. Suddenly, the steady drone of voices was silenced. A belligerent drunkard called Dray began to expound boisterously on God's wrath at Sodom and Gomorrah.

"Those sodomizin', worthless people in that wicked city got what they deserved. Justice will be served when they're all rotting in hell."

In the moment, I was at that table, but I still felt myself standing on the edge of the large pit of festering corpses. My mind, consumed in darkness, teetered on the precipice of reason when Dray swaggered about and made his comments.

I can't remember what happened after I rose to my feet. When I came to myself, I was being held on the floor by many hands. Dray lay bloody and beaten on the floor of the tavern.

I considered myself passive, having never lifted a hand against any man. But I now had a reputation I neither wanted nor recalled. Dray survived the beating, but the memory of my exploding anger frightened me of myself.

My friend Jacob, the town constable at this time, arrested me. He hauled me out of the tavern, pushing down on my shoulders to lower my head, so I might pass through the door. For the first time, I saw an apprehension, almost fear, on the faces of the onlookers.

He put me in a cell overnight, explaining it was for my own protection.

Embracing reputations I have not earned is one of my life's great regrets. Such reputations seem to appeal to a young man. Without the wisdom that comes with age, a man will allow pride, vanity, and ego to control his mind. A young man will willingly accept that violence should be a part of his life. In my youth, at times, I would feel a sick craving to find the places and people to fill this primal need. Looking back, I never felt I deserved the good life inherited from my parents. Perhaps this was my penance.

Over the next year, I felt anxiety, waiting for Dray's reprisal. It never came. The fact is at Blood's Tavern, what I did was commonplace. My new reputation seemed to be held in the minds of those in town who knew me and heard of the incident after I was released from jail.

The day after putting my parents to rest and spending the night in jail, I rented a mule and returned to St. Joseph to recover their belongings. Even under the risk of Yellow Fever, looters driven by greed were landing their boats on the shores of St. Joseph, stealing what they could, and slipping away before detection or contagion. My father's business was in ruins, looted and burned. I was fortunate my parent's home had not yet been the target of looters and ruffians.

I tied my rented mule to the hitching post in front. My entire body trembled as I walked toward the house. I felt lightheaded as I turned the key, opened the door, and stepped inside. The smell of my mother's perfume overwhelmed me. I fell to the floor, weeping bitterly.

I eventually regained my composure and got on with the task of collecting the family possessions. These would be the items my parents considered precious: my father's books he taught me from, my mother's jewelry that had been passed down from generation to generation, our family Bibles which carried the written record of our heritage, and my father's strong box that lay hidden in a space beneath the floorboards. Only my parents and I knew the hiding place.

Loading the remnants of their lives onto my father's wagon, I retrieved the mule, harnessed him to the wagon, and began the journey back to Apalachicola. On the seat beside me, I kept my father's matched set of Colt Paterson revolvers and an old saber he'd hung on the wall of his study. Although I was a poor shot and would not have considered myself an asset in a gunfight, I felt the sight of the armaments might discourage any highwaymen I might encounter.

It was a quiet trip, and I saw no signs of human life during the journey. At points, the path became the shoreline of the bay. I stopped to rest the mule. Out over the green and blue water, the sun started to paint a beautiful mosaic in the early evening sky, and a breeze drifted in off the Gulf.

For the first time all day, I felt as though I could breathe. Here in this beautiful place, I wondered how a tragedy so horrendous could have happened. Then, in a moment of clarity, I was overwhelmed by a sense of my own insignificance. I felt the vastness of creation and could no longer imagine myself at its center.

With or without me, the tides would ebb and rise, the sun would ascend and set, and life would go on. I could hear the voice of my mother reciting Matthew 6:26.

> "Behold the fowls of the air: for they sow not, neither do they reap, nor gather into barns; yet your heavenly Father feedeth them. Are ye not much better than they?"

I felt great comfort in this verse. Perhaps I was not alone. I recited the verse, using it to guide me through the hard times.

My father was a prudent man who lived well within his means. His strong box contained an impressive sum in gold and silver coin, and an account book from a bank in Boston, which held the bulk of his savings. The deed to his home in St. Joseph showed clear title, and there was a deed to a small holding of lands in Boston, inherited from my mother's family.

Father built a nice home in St. Joseph—a home that now sat in a ghost town. I contracted with a company to bring the house by barge to Apalachicola.

The house from St. Joseph was put on the corner of Cedar Street and Columbus, just beside the old home place on Laurel, both houses looking out onto Columbus Street. The Cedar house became my new home. My thought was to rent the old home place on Laurel to help secure myself a more stable financial future. I tried to think ahead as my father taught me.

It was well that I moved the house so quickly. A fire broke out in St. Joseph the day after we placed my parents' house on its new foundation. The fire, and a hurricane later that same year, added to the destruction of St. Joseph from which the town would never recover.

My decision to bring the house to Apalachicola was a wise one.

# Chapter II

## The Town

At six feet, five inches, I was considered by many of the time as an imposing figure, but my father at six feet, seven inches could always put my world into perspective. Many of my friends believed I missed my true calling because with the exception of my father, I was the only one in town who could light the street lamps without using a step stool. I attribute my height to the German side of my family. Growing up in a mostly German family, I became conversational in German, and because of a close friend who came each year to work the shipping season, I picked up some Portuguese, which enabled me to converse with the people who lived in the Italian community. At times, I interpreted for local businessmen. The Latin I had learned in school seemed of little use, and after a few years would begin to fade from my mind.

In the early 1800s, the Forbes Company—formerly Panton and Leslie Company—became the one firm in the Spanish territory allowed to represent Spain in the fur-trading industry.

In 1804, with the consent of the Spanish government, a land grant was approved, transferring 1.2 million acres of Creek Indian land to the Forbes Company for the payment of Indian debt owed to its trading posts. The land transfer was later called the Forbes Purchase.

The Spanish territory of Florida was transferred to the United States in July of 1821, I was born one year later in July 1822; my father once told me the two events were more than likely not connected.

The rights to the Forbes Purchase were transferred to businessmen and politicians of New York who saw potential in the land grant. The government in Washington was plagued by the transfer and became so flooded by requests for Spanish land grants that a commission was set up to deny title to all land grants purchased or conferred before the territory became a part of the United States.

The investors in the Forbes Purchase went to court and spent nearly twenty years fighting for the rights to claim the land. In 1835, after the rich of the northeast had time to prepare to exploit the prosperity created by a new port town, Washington approved the grant, and the Forbes Company took title. The Forbes Company soon after changed its name to the Apalachicola Land Company feeling the name Apalachicola would be better accepted by the locals.

People living on the land thought they had squatter's rights and would buy the land after five years for one dollar and fifty cents per acre. When the new firm took over, the squatters found their property and personal possessions seized by the Apalachicola Land Company and put up for sale at the first company auction in 1836

Many of the people of the area did not want to be a part of the monopoly that would become the Apalachicola Land Company. Some traveled twenty miles west and formed the city of St. Joseph. They built their town on one of the deepest harbors on the Gulf coast and were soon making plans to steal Apalachicola's cotton trade. The rivalry between the towns became bitter and did not end until the destruction of St. Joseph by Yellow Fever and the hurricane of 1841.

The Apalachicola Land Company dredged the Apalachicola River channel in 1836—one of their first improvements. This marked the first time a ship drafting twelve feet could come right to the wharves in town. Ships drafting fifteen feet could come within seven and a half miles. Larger ships anchored sometimes as much as six miles off the barrier islands of St. George or St. Vincent. Steamers transferred cargo and passengers to and from the ships off shore.

From 1828—when the first steamer Fannie made its way up the river to Columbus, Georgia—to 1860, over one hundred and thirty steamers serviced the Apalachicola River. Of the one hundred thirty, sixty-four called Apalachicola their home port. Adding the number of steamers from other ports, there were times it appeared possible for a person to jump from riverboat to riverboat and make it all the way to Columbus, Georgia.

Twenty steamers were built in shipyards up-river; eight were built right here in Apalachicola. About thirteen of them were stern-wheelers. Most were side-wheelers, which were more efficient and maneuverable on the meandering river system.

In the best of years, the river rose in December and stayed up—with the bulk of the cotton shipped before April. Because the water level of the river couldn't be depended on, the season usually ran from December to June. If the river didn't rise, there would be no cotton-shipping season.

Sailors and transients swarmed into the town to find seasonal work. The season could increase Apalachicola's population to near five thousand.

Our largest community was Irish town, down near the Florida Promenade in Live Oak Grove. It went in this order: Irish, German, British, Italian, and Greek. At times, during the early years, you rarely heard English spoken on our streets. Off-season, under the threat of Yellow Fever, our population could drop to fewer than a hundred.

To ask the locals what they thought of themselves and their town was to imagine a Philadelphia or Boston sitting on the Gulf Coast.

In 1833, an engineer sent by the Forbes Company came to lay out a city plan. The names of our streets and the layout of our squares and parks resembled the engineer's home town of Philadelphia. The Forbes Company required that in order to maintain a cosmopolitan waterfront, cotton warehouses be built identical, brick, thirty foot by eighty foot, three stories tall, with French doors in front, framed in granite pillars. The granite was quarried in Quincy, Massachusetts, and sent down as ballast on ships.

In December of 1838, the *Apalachicola Gazette* boasted of our superior town in an article.

The river is riz—the boat bells are ringing, ships
are loading, draymen swearing, negroes singing,

19

clerks marking, captains busy, merchants selling, packages rolling, boxes tumbling, wares rumbling, and everybody appears to be up to his eyes in business.

I took a walk up Water Street this morning for the purpose of taking a birds-eye view of the busy world, learning the news, and so on. On one of the wharves I saw a steam-boat captain, and I thought I would learn something of the up country from him.

'What's the news up country, Captain?'

'Step aboard the boat Sir—off in five minutes—Loaded down to the guards—fare only twenty dollars to Columbus — will you walk aboard?'

'Guess not Sir,' and walking on a short distance, I met a dry goods dealer.

'Good morning, Sir.'

'Twenty thousand.'

'Twenty thousand what, Sir?' said I astonished.

'Twenty thousand dollars' worth of goods I've sold this morning,' and away he went.

'Well—thinks I, these are queer times. I can't get a civil answer from anyone it appears. Just then, I saw a farmer passing by. Guess I'll get some news this time; that man isn't crazy, and walking up to him—

'What is the news in your section stranger?'

'Five hundred and eleven and three-eighths.'

'Five hundred thunders! What do you mean?'

'Why I sold five hundred bales of cotton this morning, but you needn't be in such a passion about it. I reckon you won't have to pay for it.'

The fact is, Apalachicola is herself again. The bales, boxes, packages, and cotton with which our wharves are crowded, with the cheerful hum of business is enough to make glad the heart of any man who loves the air of prosperity.

By 1860, we had built so many cotton warehouses—numbering near sixty—some called us "The Granite Forest." We didn't look at ourselves as a rough and hardened frontier town but rather through the eyes of the future and the town we would become. We could see no end to the prosperity.

I remember the eighth Census of the United States ordered from Washington for 1860. Apalachicola had a population of one thousand nine hundred and six people, making us the sixth largest city in the state. Subtract the five hundred and twenty slaves and count the white population, and we became the third largest.

*Steamship waiting to be loaded with cotton*

An editor in a New York newspaper wrote, "During cotton shipping season, Apalachicola reminds me of a small New York City." It was not only our commerce that at times in the 1830s would rival Savannah, Georgia, but also our diversity. Apalachicola, like New York, was a melting pot, advertising in some Northern markets as a Southern city with a very Northern cosmopolitan feel.

The packet *Peytonia* held the Apalachicola record for cargo. In April of 1846, it steamed down the river with thirteen-hundred and five bales of cotton. With each bale weighing five-hundred pounds, that was 326.25 tons in cotton weight. I watched as she steamed down the river to the wharf. I climbed aboard, and from the top of the pilothouse, she was an impressive sight.

Most men of the South couldn't afford slaves. Other than the occasional lease for labor, we did our own work. Up-river plantations leased slaves to work in Apalachicola during the cotton season, and at times, the blacks staying in town would outnumber the whites.

For the most part, slaves were invisible. They were like the chair in the corner of a room or a barrel of rosin stacked in one of countless warehouses.

Growing up here during the cotton years, I never took issue with slavery. How could I have known the sin of my indifference? It was a Northern issue that started as a rumble, and by the beginning of 1861 was screaming like a steamboat whistle. This "War for Southern Independence" would impose a heavy toll on the South, our town, and our lives.

# Chapter III

## Events and Remembrances of My Youth

If asked in my youth, I would have told you I spent much of my time in study. My well-educated father believed that somewhere on the shelf between our set of *The Brockhaus' Konversations-Lexikon, 14th edition Enzyklopädie*, and the seventeen volume set of the German Bible, I would find civilized men able to create great empires. I listened closely, taking note of every word my father said, because I knew that without a doubt, my father was one of those men.

In truth, I was a good student and allowed many hours at play. My friends and I enjoyed happy days and star-filled nights exploring the Gulf Coast. With wooden sabers, we searched swamplands around town for the last of the hostile Creek Indians that may have slipped past Andy Jackson. Our Indians stayed to themselves in peace. We grew up hearing stories of the great Seminole war, stories that found their way into our games. Creatures, commonplace here, would amaze friends and family on my visits to Boston, making me the center of attention at family dinners.

Hatch Wefing and Jacob Foley were my good friends. Growing up in a port town, many friends would come and go, but Hatch and Jacob were always there for me, as I was for them. Hatch's father, a steamboat captain, entrusted by the Callahan line to operate several of their steamers, carried passengers and freight up and down the river. Hatch was a gifted storyteller. He had access to all the best information, gleaning it from sailors who came to our town from ports far away.

Hatch explained that adults, so as not to cause a panic, kept his stories out of the papers. He said they thought since there was no escaping a foreboding destiny, it was best to allow the children to live in ignorance. Hatch would take the stories and embellish them, twisting the details until they became our stories. Jacob and I were never surprised to learn that in the deep water off Fort Brooke in the bay of Tampa, a ship spotted a Kraken attempting to pull a coastal schooner into the watery depths.

Even closer to home, one foggy night on a sandbar just below Chattahoochee, the crew of the riverboat *Steubenville* chained themselves to the rail of the steamer to prevent a gathering of sirens from calling them to a certain watery grave.

We especially liked his tales after a storm because we knew that somewhere, some ship's captain would cross paths with the *Flying Dutchman*. This doomed ship, crewed by the victims of the dread Yellow Jack, glowed with an eerie light—a light generated from the very recesses of Hell itself. He could tell the stories with a conviction that would make you feel as though they were real.

To meet Hatch's father was to see that the seed did not fall far from the tree. There were nights on the porch at Hatch's home where his father, a man I would describe as a grizzled, old seaman, spun tales that kept us awake and looking over our shoulders for hours.

I would describe Jacob as being steadfast. Whereas Hatch and I believed the stories could be true, Jacob tried to believe in an attempt to escape the reality that was his life. I failed to believe anything really scared Jacob though. There were times when the three of us would camp along the river. Late at night with the fire burning dim, we spun our tales, with imaginations running wild. There was always a strange sound in the night. Hatch and I stiffened like statues, but not Jacob. Jacob would rise and walk away from the fire into the night, stand briefly to let his eyes become accustomed to the dark, and search for the cause of the noise. Hatch and I, cowering near the area of darkness and light, would call out, "Do you see anything? What is it?"

Jacob's father Brian was described as a good man and a hard worker. He was part owner in a turpentine camp and was standing too close to the still when it exploded and killed him.

Jacob's mother's family from New York believed she married beneath her station. They sent enough money to help support the grieving widow and her young son. Miss Jenny used the money to purchase and start Jenny House, a boardinghouse, and struggled to make it a success. The boardinghouse supported Jacob and his mother, and twice I can remember them making the long journey to visit their family near Syracuse.

Say what you may about Brian Foley; the truth was, he instilled in Jacob a strong sense of responsibility. Jacob worked on the docks at an early age. He was no stranger to hard labor. To bump into Jacob on the street was like running into one of the granite pillars that framed the doors of the cotton warehouses.

My father held a position of respect. He was entrusted with the records involved in the comings and goings of shipping into our port town. He was frequently asked to sit for the town council or serve on one of many committees. Our social lives centered on the activities of the Trinity Episcopal Church. Sunday services started at eight in the morning and ended at noon. After their noon meal, the congregation would once again drift back to the churchyard to discuss religion and politics. The evening service began at six and ran until the Vicar finished.

My mother was a genteel woman who embodied all the finest qualities that define a true, Southern lady. In the kitchen, she had no equal, and the ladies of the town would often ask her advice on culinary matters. She was a seamstress, doctor, and advisor to her young son, many times demonstrating the faith and patience of Job. She taught through parable and example, never raising her voice, able to persevere when all around her lost hope. To my father, she was the air he breathed. He said that without her he would die.

Sometimes the steel in a man becomes too hot, and he loses his reason. I would see this repeatedly in our town when a man walked away in disgust, cursing and vowing no resolution, ready to fight and die in the defense of a cause not worthy of these extremes. Women like my mother would hold these men and whisper the words capable of quenching the fire that tempered the steel. It was in the arms of these amazing women that men would find resolutions. My father may have been the undisputed head of our family, but my mother was our center.

I was five when a tiny hand reached out from a fold in a blanket my mother held in her arms. This tiny hand appeared to extend out to me and for a brief moment grasped my finger, then released it, as my baby brother passed from this world. I remember my mother and father placing him in a round, wooden hatbox. They buried him under the magnolia tree behind the house. My mother wept as my father tried to explain to me that the baby came too soon. I visited my brother many times over the years, sitting under the tree, telling him of my adventures and how sometimes in my dreams, he and I played together.

***

Old Hickory was a 'gator of legendary proportions. Like the General Andrew Jackson with the nickname, he was aggressive and never backed down. Hickory was usually out on the river around the slaughterhouse north of town and from time to time was sighted early in the morning near the town market. He liked it when the merchants, while preparing for the new day's market, threw the old meat and produce from the stands into the river.

Old Hickory always seemed able to stay out of range of would-be captors. Stories spread of his ability to dismantle traps, sometimes ripping giant cypress trees right out of the riverbank to escape a snare. The best guess was eighteen feet. People attempting a more accurate measurement didn't return.

When I was eleven, fishing with my friends at the city dock, I straddled one of the pilings that held the dock in place. I tied my line around the piling. On occasion, I would hold the line in my hands or pick the line up on my foot, holding it between my toes to check the tug, pull of a bite. I leaned forward and gazed down at the surface of the river some five feet below. I saw my image in the water and watched the reflection of white clouds passing overhead. At times, it made me feel as though I was moving. Forcing my eyes to focus just beneath the surface, I could just make out the first couple of fish tied to my stringer.

We were laughing and telling stories of our exploits when all of a sudden, it appeared as though my stringer of fish began to rise on one of the reflected clouds. Before I could blink, Old Hickory with his mouth gaping open, rose from the depths as though fired from a cannon.

Vertically, about eight feet out of the water, he rose. His belly, white and checkered, became a solid wall, inches from my face. I gripped the piling as his great mass continued to rise before me. The power lifted me up, trying to throw me back, and I gripped the piling tighter. Then, in my moment of greatest fear, I saw my left leg bent and from the knee down, rising from one side of Hickory's jaw, my stringer of fish hung from the other side. He reached the pinnacle of his rise, then opened his jaws for a brief moment and flipped his head to one side. He snapped the stringer of fish into his mouth. As he slung the fish for a better hold and just before he snapped, my leg fell free. My friends said if not for the piling, Hickory would have swallowed me up and into that great belly of his.

Before the alligator could fall back to the water, Jacob rushed up, pulled me back, and held me firm. I leaned on Jacob while Hatch and the others ran yelling to the merchants on the waterfront.

Old Hickory didn't break the skin, but he dislocated my knee. Jacob reassured me, "Don't fret Michael; you can still win our bet." Most of the men of our town had at some point lost body parts, sometimes arms and legs. Most of the time, it was just a few joints on a couple of fingers. Jacob, Hatch, and I had bet that we could keep ours. An earlier accident took Jacob out of the running. He lost three joints on his left hand when a cart carrying a five-hundred-pound bale of cotton rolled over it.

Hatch retrieved my father from the Customs House, and both came running. As he ran down the dock, Hatch yelled out, "Is he alive? Is he alive?" My father picked me up in his arms and carried me down the street to the Post Office.

Dr. John Gorrie had arrived earlier that same year and was working as assistant postmaster. He worked the additional job until people of the town gave credence to the medical profession and paid him in coin rather than barter.

Father put me on the counter. Up to this point, I experienced very little pain. Dr. Gorrie examined the injury to my knee, pointing out to my father how fortunate I was to escape with my life. The knee carried the mark of a tooth on both sides but Old Hickory must have been missing teeth where my knee passed through his jaw. If he chomped down a few inches higher on my leg, or if my knee had not bent, Hickory would have lifted me off the dock and pulled me under, for a much different outcome.

Dr. Gorrie mixed Laudanum with a small amount of brandy and insisted I swallow it. The mixture was strong and bitter which caused me to choke. It took two attempts to finish the small glass.

My father stayed at my shoulder, held me against the counter, and told me to be brave. My head started to spin, and my senses dulled because of the potent brew, but still I felt very little pain. Dr. Gorrie told my father to brace himself, and in one quick movement, the joint of my knee popped back into place. The sound and pain still lives in my memories.

Friends and locals who gathered to watch through the open windows, gasped at the sound. Hatch told me later two of the women fainted when the joint fell back into place. I survived and became the envy of my friends who later told me it was the most amazing sight they had ever witnessed. I was written into the Old Hickory legend. If not for the pain, it had been a good day for a boy of eleven. With that said, my father smiled, and my mother strongly disagreed. Over time, the pain left my knee, but it became stiff and unyielding, and I walked with poor cadence.

One thing you could say about Old Hickory is he had a lot of character. I did not believe all the stories about him. He received blame for every bad happening on the river. It is not possible that Hickory could have been in all those places at the same time.

We believed this was one of the finest places in the world to grow up. Even while in Boston for a visit, after a few days, I became homesick. Frontier was the word to describe us, and the rules of surviving in a coastal frontier were second nature to us. Obey the rules, and live a long life. Breaking the rules could result in premature death, sometimes quick, and sometimes agonizingly slow and painful.

Alligators were one of the obvious threats. We treated them with respect and gave them a wide berth. They could be avoided, and, when cooked properly, made a very good meal. The general rule was that no matter whether it was a plant or an animal, if it could stab you, stick you, or bite you, it was more than likely poisonous. Although it may not kill you, it could make you wish you were dead.

Scorpions and black widows had to be purged from the house periodically. When moving objects around outside, it was best to be on the lookout for timber, diamondback, and pygmy rattlesnakes. Turpentine workers wore a piece of stovepipe between their shoes and their knees to avoid the deadly bite of these snakes. One of the more dangerous snakes found everywhere, but mainly near the river in the marsh grass, was the cottonmouth water moccasin.

Most snakes would put out a warning, as if to say stay away, and if you left them alone, they would simply crawl away. Cottonmouth water moccasins were aggressive, and at times when we were near the water, they would approach us.

When we traveled out into the bay, the jellyfish and stingrays could give us a nasty pain, but we all knew the real danger just below the surface was sharks. Sharks of large proportion cruised the Gulf and bay and the deep passes at the ends of the islands. Some of the sharks, like bull sharks, were able to tolerate the fresh water. These were the worst of the group and could often be seen traveling up the river to the slaughterhouse. Here, they competed with alligators for carcasses of the butchered animals. Only the largest 'gators, like Old Hickory, stayed in the areas where sharks patrolled.

These creatures appeared to us to be mindless, with one thought—feeding. They had black eyes and no conscience, and while most predators backed down to avoid a crippling injury, sharks would aggressively attack with no regard for their own welfare. A large shark would generally make the initial attack. Once there was blood in the water, the smaller sharks swarmed in and finished off the helpless victim.

When I heard of a disappearance on the river, I always suspected sharks. Sharks, one of my deepest fears, were frequently in my nightmares. Panthers, black bears, and wolves filled the swamps around town. These creatures were given names that revealed their cunning nature. They became a part of local folklore and legend. From a young age, I noticed that when seamen would speak of sharks, an ancient fear entered, adding a slight tremble to their voices.

Stories of sharks were never about the triumph of men, their attempts to trap them, or the great shot that took down the beast, but rather the story about how much of the victim's body, if any, could be recovered and speculation on the size of the shark.

As youths, my friends and I traveled the old Indian paths past the slaughterhouse to sandbars where we felt safe to enjoy the river.

The largest irritation in our lives came from the smallest of our creatures—insects at times would appear as clouds rising from the swampland. Although they posed no real threat, their sheer number could push a man to the edge of insanity. Some, like the no-see-ums, passed through the finest gauze fabric and feasted while you slept. Mosquitoes, at times, were a plague. They fed mostly in the early morning and night—always in greatest numbers during the Yellow Fever outbreaks, adding an unwanted irritation to the death and misery.

Each type of insect had its own season. When one would vanish, another would appear in its place: mosquitoes, biting gnats, dog flies, green heads, yellow flies, and deer flies all lined up for a feast. After a long hot summer, we looked forward to the fall and winter, when the onslaught would end, and the cool weather would give us a well-deserved break.

I have seen the face of Yellow Fever rear its ugly head, time and time again. Bluish patches covered jaundiced, yellow skin, and the urine became dark and reddish. It was common to bleed from the eyes, ears, gums, and nose. Victims suffered from severe headaches, backaches, and nausea. The worst was the black vomit—expelled from the mouth, the stomach contents resembled coffee grounds. After four to ten days, the victim became comatose and died. This was a disease of nightmares.

*"Dragging down Florida"*
*Yellow Fever, nicknamed Yellow Jack.*

# Chapter IV

## Pawns of War

It is my sincere belief that politics, religion, and commerce are indeed the three great evils of the world. I also believe that no matter where I travel, if I go out among the common people, they will accept me. The basic instinct of people is to survive, raise a family, and make life better for their children. However, when politics, religion, and commerce enter into the equation, they open the door to the sins of pride, greed, and lust for power—the handmaidens of war.

Little did I know in 1861 that my encounter with Old Hickory years earlier would more than likely save my life later. Even though I was a member of the Franklin Guards, because of my crippled leg, the Confederate Army did not consider me a candidate able to meet the requirements of a Confederate soldier. Near forty years old and considered crippled, I was to be left behind.

Hatch, following his father's footsteps, was one of the best pilots on the Apalachicola River. His skills as a riverboat pilot were also his greatest value to the Confederacy.

Confederate command insisted he take a deferment and continue moving troops and supplies between Columbus, Georgia, and the coastal ports. I would see Hatch several times during the war on one of his many river journeys, and after hearing the news from upriver, I would spend sleepless nights worried about my friend.

The industrial economy of the North had nothing in common with the agricultural society of the South. Slavery for the most part did not affect the lives of most Southern families who worked hard just trying to eke out a living.

Slavery was, however, an issue, especially to the Southern aristocracy. The fact is, you did not have to go too far north to find men of power and position, willing to take advantage of Apalachicola's economy.

Throughout the 1830s and 1840s, plantation owners from Alabama and Georgia came to Apalachicola, setting up slaves in our town. These slaves lived unsupervised, married, raising families, and they rented themselves out as laborers. They appeared to live as free men with one exception: as much as eighty percent of their earnings went back to their masters in Alabama and Georgia.

This angered some of the businessmen and other white citizens of Apalachicola. In the late 1840s, the same white citizens of Apalachicola began to grumble, "These black men walk around town like they're free, which results in drunks, fights, and murders on the streets of Apalachicola." This, of course, was far from the truth. What they were really saying was they didn't like slave masters from Alabama and Georgia coming to our town to set up their slaves, reaping enormous profits, and taking the money out of town. To the people of Apalachicola, these slave masters were no better than, "Damn Yankees."

Along about 1849, the city passed ordinances requiring a slave owner or an associate of the owner to live on the property with his slaves, putting an end to some of these abuses. I supposed that slavery could be a hard life, whether on a plantation of cotton, tobacco, indigo, or sugarcane, but here in Apalachicola, black faces were overlooked because of the premium put on labor. It was not until the war that I realized how much I took freedom for granted.

I spent several nights trying to convince my friend Jacob not to enlist. I did my best to persuade him that the issues, as presented, were not as cut and dried as the politicians let on. In this war, there was no right or wrong, no clear black or white, just many shades of gray.

Jacob believed in the words of Dr. Gorrie who as early mayor of Apalachicola said, "It is one of the worst cases of absenteeism that ever bankrupted a country." Gorrie referred to businessmen from the north coming to our port town during the height of the cotton shipping season, reaping enormous profits, then boarding steamers headed back to the north to spend their money…money that would be better spent here in Apalachicola.

Jacobs's family was for the most part Irish, which in many places put him just above being black. He was, however, one hundred percent Apalachicolan. He had a very basic education. He could read and understand the gist of a story, could write, but struggled with spelling and grammar.

He told me, "You don't have to be a theologian to have religious faith, and you don't have to understand all reasons for the war. Just have faith in the leadership." This is a faith that I did not possess.

Jacob's sense of patriotism won out, and he signed up for the Confederate Army. There was no minimum age enforced, but you had to be thirty-five or under to enlist. Jacob lied about his age claiming he was thirty-four although he was nearer thirty-eight. Much to my chagrin, officials either believed him or didn't care, and he got away with his lie.

As the war progressed, with human carnage increasing and human resources depleted, the requirement would be raised to fifty, and by the end of the war, a warm body was the only standard.

Jacob enlisted in the Florida First Infantry Company B, a temporary one-year regiment. Company B mustered at Chattahoochee then transferred to Pensacola. At the end of his enlistment, he re-enlisted in the reorganized Florida First Infantry Company K for another three years.

Jacob was an unquestioning Confederate soldier, the perfect Confederate soldier. He firmly believed in the right of the South to secede from the Union but had a hard time putting those feelings into words.

It occurs to me that in every war, on each side, there are two soldiers: the son of the rich and the son of the poor. The rich man's son was offered different types of deferment, even to the extent of hiring a substitute to replace himself in the ranks; thereby he once again evaded service in the Confederate forces. The Confederate Congress amended the draft, exempting any man owning over twenty slaves—an amendment clearly passed to protect the privileged sons of wealthy plantation owners.

Then I looked at the manure of war and saw the gun fodder, the poor men's sons. They were the first to step forward to serve for a cause they vaguely understood, and they were willing to defend the cause with their lives. There would be no deferment for the sons of the poor.

The sons of the Southern aristocracy who served advanced quickly, taking their place in the command structure as officers even though they did not possess the disciplines to deserve the rank. I shudder to think of the number of soldiers who died under the command of arrogant, unqualified officers.

Jacob became well known throughout his company and notorious to the Northern forces they battled. He was one of the few rebels to carry a price on his head. Jacob fashioned a short club out of hickory. On one side, near the tip, he embedded the sharpened steel outline of a three-leaf clover, a design he took from a deck of cards. On the other side, he embedded a sharpened steel blade made from a large "bastard" file. He carried this club in his right hand, and the broken remains of a Cavalry saber in his left. After the initial shots, these became the tools of his trade as he engaged the enemy in hand-to-hand combat. He fought all of the major engagements in the Western War Theater. Fighting with Braxton Bragg's Army of the Tennessee, he fought at Shiloh and Stones River, leaving the imprint of the King of Clubs on those who stood in his way. There was no way we could actually confirm the hero was Jacob, and although reports suggested it was, I could hardly imagine it.

Secession took place on January 10, 1861. We were the third state to secede from the Union. However, we did not learn of this for several days, having to wait for the news to travel.

We were a sparsely populated state adding a small number of men to the Confederate forces. We were, however, a state surrounded by water, and with so much coastline and so many ports, the Union found it impossible to blockade all of the possible entry points.

Our role in the war effort was to maintain the supply lines. Cattle and salt would become two of the state's largest contributions to the Confederate cause. I felt, like many people, that the war would be short-lived, and after a few months, life would return to normal, whether as part of the United States or as part of the new Confederate States.

***

On the evening of Wednesday, April 10, 1861, after a long day at the Customs House, I was sitting on a bench in the bowery on Water Street. I looked across at the row of taverns opening the doors for the evening trade. I was weary of thinking and contemplated going in to try to dull my senses. However, as the fates would have it, this would be the night I would meet LaRaela Retsyo Agnusdei.

My mind was racing with thoughts, and as I stared blindly ahead with no focus, I suddenly realized there was a presence before me. A little girl, who appeared to be all of seven years old, stood at the tips of my boots and curtsied.

"Evening, Mr. Brandon. How are you this evening, Mr. Brandon?"

"Hello, fine, thanks," I replied.

"You're welcome," she replied, in a bold little voice. She promptly moved to my left side and sat down on the bench as if we were old acquaintances.

"You don't know me, but I know you. My friends in town tell me you're a good man, that I can trust you. My name is LaRaela Retsyo Agnusdei, but you can call me Pearl," she said.

"Nice to meet you, Pearl," I replied.

"My mama picked my name. It's a riddle. She left me a letter that said someday I would figure out why she called me Pearl, and I just know that someday I'll figure it out."

"I'm sure you will," I said. Confused, I stared at Pearl. I puzzled why this child whom I had seen around town, but not heard, suddenly decided to strike up a conversation.

"I have a Pearl. Would you like to see it?" Before I could speak, she pulled a chain from beneath her collar, and on the chain was a small oddly-shaped Pearl.

"This is what my mama left me. She put it around my neck when I was born. You see, I was born in Mississippi, and those oysters over

36

there don't just make round pearls. They come in different shapes. I always wear my necklace 'cause it reminds me of my mama. I never met my mama, and some say she was a gypsy, but I don't believe that. I'm waiting on my papa. He comes down here all the time to get his medicine. I don't think it's really medicine. I think it's what they call rum. He said it helps him forget that I killed my mama."

With a confounded look on my face, I shook my head, indicating I didn't believe in her guilt.

Pearl continued, "I know that's probably not true 'cause the Vicar says it was just what they call a coincidence that my mama died the same day I was born. I think that's probably the truth 'cause the Vicar works for God, and everybody knows you can't lie and work for God. He's a good man. Do you know the Vicar?"

I could not have gotten a word in edgewise, so I just nodded my head, acknowledging that I knew the Vicar.

"The Vicar and I are good friends," said Pearl. "We sit all the time speakin' about all the goings-on in town. When I'm waiting down here for my papa, I have another nickname. I bet you can't guess in a hundred years what people down here call me?

"Give me a clue," I told her.

"They call me Prickly Pear." She didn't seem to even stop to take a breath.

"Sometimes the men folk drink too much medicine, and it can make them act strange so I keep some jackknives sewn into my petticoats. If they get out of hand, I just stick 'em. The troublemakers have learned to leave me alone or they'll get poked, and nobody wants to be poked by the Prickly Pear.

"But don't you worry Mr. Brandon, everybody tells me you're a good man, and I would never find cause to poke you. My papa once sent me to live with my aunt, my mama's sister. I think he hoped she'd keep me, but I heard her talking about how homely I was, and how she didn't think I would fit in with her beautiful daughters. That's why I wear the pretty dresses. I think it makes me easier to look at. Do you think my dress is pretty Mr. Brandon?"

"Why yes, you and your dress," I replied.

"Oh thank you for saying so, Mr. Brandon. Don't worry, I don't think you can go to hell for telling white lies if they're meant to make people feel better. I don't care that I'm not very pretty. Vicar says God only cares if I'm clean and polite, and he says he knows I do my best. Vicar says that God takes care of them little bitty sparrows, make'n sure they get all they need, and he loves me a lot more than he loves a sparrow. I figure I've got that going for me too. Do you think that's true, Mr. Brandon?"

"Happens to be one of my favorite verses in the Bible," I replied.

"You know, sometimes I go down to the Florida House and visit with Miss Caroline. She is very kind, and sometimes when my papa doesn't come home, she lets me eat with her boarders there at the Florida House Restaurant. She's a real good cook. Sometimes when I visit her, we sit in the morning and have a tea or some breakfast, and we see you walk'n by on your way to work. 'There goes that nice looking Mr. Brandon,' Miss Caroline always tells me. 'He should take his meals here at the restaurant. I could put some meat on those bones,' she tells me."

I looked at my arm. Maybe I was a little skinny.

"She's a nice lady. She said she lost her husband three years ago, but I never seen her lookin' for him, so he must be lost good, 'cause I think Miss Caroline has given up find'n him. Do you know Miss Caroline?"

I nodded my head yes and replied, "But not very well."

"You'd like her a lot; she's pretty and a real good cook."

"I'd heard she was a good cook."

"This is my newest dress. I know it's a little big, but Miss Sadie says I'll grow into it."

Suddenly she switched people on me. I had just focused on Miss Caroline.

"Miss Sadie and her mama, Miss Annie, have been very kind to me. Miss Sadie is all the time giving me new dresses that she had left over from when she was a little girl. Sometimes they fix my hair, and I know it's a sin, but I think it makes me real pretty."

"I've met Miss Annie and Miss Sadie," I told her.

38

"Miss Sadie and I have the most wonderful talks about everything and everybody. Sometimes, Miss Annie, Miss Sadie's mama, will throw her hands in the air and tell Miss Sadie, 'Don't be so incorrigible.' And she'll just walk right out of the room into the kitchen. We still know she's there 'cause we can hear her chuckling."

"Miss Charity is my best friend. She is what I would imagine my mama would be like if she hadn't died. She teaches me to cook and take care of myself. She gives me a bath once a week. Miss Charity helps me wash and keep my dresses clean and pressed."

Another woman. Confound her. What is she up to?

"She's not free though. She belongs to Miss Sadie's grandpa, Mr. Thomas Orman. Miss Charity, she's the most beautiful color of black. The Vicar said the way I live I must have a guardian angel watching over me. I think he's right, and I just know it's Miss Charity."

She stood up and curtsied. "It's sure been nice talkin' to you, Mr. Brandon, but you'll have to excuse me. I got to go find Miss Charity, or she'll be worried about me. Are you here to get some medicine?"

"No, I was just resting before I headed home. It was very nice meeting you."

Pearl smiled and said, "Goodnight, Mr. Brandon."

Smiling back, I said, "Goodnight, Pearl."

Pearl was a fixture in town, appearing in different places and engaging anyone who walked by. She presented herself in full dress as though going to a party. Her dresses were generally clean but well worn. Only a couple of times did I see her in a dress that was not too large or too small. Pearl was thin as a rail, and God forgive me for saying so, but a bit homely.

There were so many out-of-proportion features on that child's face that when she spoke, her expressions endeared her to you. I guess the best way to describe Pearl would be to compare her to a baby manatee with features so out of the ordinary she became cute.

Pearl excelled in personality. People went out of their way to speak to her because no matter how big your own troubles, little Pearl's life put your own life back in perspective. As tough as Pearl's life was, she didn't know any better. She accepted it and attacked life with an overwhelming spirit—a spirit I found contagious.

*Orman House. Sadie Orman, lower left; Annie Orman, upper porch; Sarah Orman, lower porch; Jacob Kohler said his father Michael Kohler had told him the young girl might be Pearl and that the black man could be William Marr.*

After speaking to Pearl, I no longer felt the need to go to the taverns that night. I returned home, sat on the porch, and thought about what Pearl's life must be like. After a while, I started thinking about Caroline down at the Florida Boarding House. I'd had lady friends in the past— they would come and go—but I never thought of myself as the courting type. Because I felt large and awkward most of my life, perhaps women sensed how I felt about myself, and my lack of confidence reflected back in the way they felt about me.

By 1861, more states seceded from the Union, a Confederate government was set up, and federal forts in the South fell to Union forces. With all of this going on, it seemed hard to find the time to visit Miss Caroline at the Florida House Restaurant.

Two days after speaking to Pearl, I was bathed and groomed, smelling like a dandy, approaching the Florida Boarding House restaurant. I told myself, "It's not a big deal. I'm just going for a meal." Miss Caroline simply ran a boarding house and an eating establishment that catered to all who walked in. I intended to try the food, and this just happened to be the night I decided to go, and that was all there was to it.

On the steps to the porch, my head began to spin and my legs became weak. I peered through the open door and saw six, small, round tables with four chairs at each table. There were customers at three of the tables. This was good for me since had all of the tables been occupied, I don't think I could have dealt with it.

Pearl's smiling face peeked out from the partially-opened kitchen door before it swung shut. My instincts told me to flee, but I found myself frozen in place as Caroline entered the room. I hadn't realized until that moment how beautiful she was. How is it I had not noticed her in the past? She was twenty-seven Pearl had said. I questioned whether this was really happening. What could she possibly see in me?

She swept across the room as though she were dancing. "Why, Mr. Brandon, welcome to the Florida House Restaurant. Will you be joining us for dinner?"

I must have responded, but to this day, I could swear on a Bible that I did not utter a word. Gripping me by my hand and elbow, she led me to the corner table, indicating the seat facing the room. "You do remember me, don't you Mr. Brandon? We met at a church social a couple of years ago."

"Oh, yes, I remember," I lied.

Before I could speak another word, Caroline said, "I hope you brought your appetite; so many wonderful things are cooking in the kitchen tonight." With that said, she dashed across the floor and into the kitchen. No sooner had Caroline disappeared then Pearl re-entered with a tray filled with over two dozen oysters. Placing them in front of me, she smiled.

"Good evening Mr. Brandon. I hope you enjoy your meal." The words had barely left her mouth, and she was gone like a shot. She returned carrying a glass and pitcher. Without a word, she placed the glass on the table beside me and filled it from the pitcher. Again, she disappeared. The oysters were wonderful. They tasted of butter and garlic, and I found the ale very satisfying.

When I finished, Pearl returned, refilled my glass, and removed the platter of empty shells. At this point, I didn't know what to expect next. Pearl entered the kitchen, and before the door stopped swinging, Caroline passed through the doorway carrying three plates. I thought to myself, this must be for another table, but she walked toward me.

With the three plates before me, she said in a voice like a song, "I hope you enjoy your meal." She smiled, turned, and walked away. I sat quietly for a moment with her smile still burning a hole in my mind, my heart pounding. I grabbed the glass of ale and drank half of it down. I unbuttoned my vest, hoping to control my perspiration. I had not moved, but I was out of breath.

Three platters of seafood held three different types of fish, each beautifully prepared, crabs, scallops, potatoes, and corn muffins. The feast was just as good as it appeared. Pearl came out regularly, refilling my glass and pitcher. I had not had a meal this satisfying in a long time.

Pearl removed the ale and soon returned with coffee and dessert—a piece of chocolate pie that rivaled those offered by the finest restaurants in Boston. Contented, I gazed around the room, noticing my table was the only one set with decorative China and real silverware. There were more plates in front of me than on tables with four guests. I was feeling uneasy when suddenly, before me stood Caroline.

"Did you enjoy your meal, Mr. Brandon?"

"Oh, yes, uh, very much." My tongue felt like it was in a knot. "I, uh, uh, can't remember the last time I had such a wonderful meal."

I found it hard to look away. Of course, it's rude to stare, but I found myself drowning in those beautiful, hazel-green eyes. I know there was a conversation, and I had to have been a part of it. Walking home, I wasn't sure what just happened, but I did know that I would be picking Caroline up where she lived at the Florida Boarding House on Sunday morning for church and that we would attend the church picnic afterward.

I awoke the next morning giddy as a schoolboy. I was the cat that ate the canary. It was not long before my thoughts turned to Pearl. I soon grasped that the seven-year-old child had sparked my interest in Caroline on purpose. Were all men as dull witted as myself? I also realized in the elation of last night's moment, I had not paid my bill.

I dressed for the day, but before leaving home, I pulled a wooden chest from the guest room closet. Inside was a box containing the contents from my mother's dresser. Sorting through the various items, I removed her silver brush and comb along with the matching hand mirror. From a smaller box, I removed a decorative glass bottle containing my mother's favorite perfume. I gathered the items and carried them to the kitchen, placing them in an old flour sack.

Prospects for my future had changed dramatically in one night. Perhaps my life would be more than just a job and an empty house. I left with bag in hand, looking forward to my next encounter with Pearl.

*** 

Little did I know at the time, that on the morning of Friday, April 12, 1861, the War for Southern Independence began with shots fired on Fort Sumter. My reasons were selfish, but I was glad it took five days for the news to travel to us. If I had known the coming events of the day, I might not have dined with Caroline.

# Chapter V

# Inconvenient Timing

In January of 1861, the cotton season ended before it began. Cotton brokers from the North came South, saw the preparations for war, and left. Troops mustered at Chattahoochee were transferred to Pensacola for reassignment. The Apalachicola River, considered a vital artery connecting the Gulf coast to Georgia and Alabama, became a center of Confederate activity as Southern forces set up blockades to secure and control river traffic. Cannon batteries brought from Pensacola were set up at the mouth of the Apalachicola River for the defense of the town. A smaller battery built on the end of St. Vincent defended West Pass.

Eighteen sixty-one found our state government in turmoil. Governor John Milton, realizing the importance of Florida ports to the Confederate effort, sent troops to defend the supply lines.

In February 1861, a convention was called in Montgomery, Alabama, at which the seven seceding states created a Confederate Constitution. Jefferson Davis was elected the first president of the Confederacy. Davis believed the capital of the Confederacy should remain in the Deep South, but other politicians of the new Southern political aristocracy found the heat of Montgomery intolerable and voted to move the new capital to Richmond, Virginia.

Much to Governor Milton's disapproval, the newly established Confederate government called for more and more Florida regiments to move into position to fight in what became the Western Theater, thus leaving Florida ports undefended and vulnerable to Union attack. December 1861 and January 1862, our batteries were disassembled and moved ninety miles up-river to Ricko's Bluff. Our troops moved north toward Tennessee. Townspeople were encouraged to evacuate. Some of us thought the war would not last long and decided to stay.

\*\*\*

On April 13, 1861, I walked with a decisive purpose. My father told me love was blinding. I never really understood that until now. With war looming on our doorstep and an uncertain future, my priority was in courting Miss Caroline. I walked to work with the step and stature of a man who must surely own the world. At each intersection, I searched for Pearl, hoping to find her sitting in one of her usual spots. I arrived at the Customs House without sighting her. With gift in hand and Pearl nowhere to be found, for the time being, I would have to quench my zeal.

The topic of conversation was the war. So many of our packet steamers were taken out of service and repurposed to move troops and supplies; it seemed as though there were few left to carry goods. With no idea of what the war could bring or how long it might last, we moved through the days with an uncertain future.

Many cotton merchants from the northeast, unwilling to take the gamble, didn't arrive for the season. Others, who found themselves surrounded by preparations for war, became apprehensive and soon left. Local citizens with Northern sympathies had already boarded steamers for passage to the northeast.

A few citizens with Northern sympathies believed as I did—the war would be short-lived—and decided to remain in Apalachicola. One example was Dr. Alvan Wentworth Chapman.

Dr. Chapman, from Southampton, Massachusetts, married a Southern woman from North Carolina. Their views on the war varied so greatly she felt the need to leave and stay with family in Marianna, Florida. Dr. Chapman remained behind and was suspected of aiding Union prisoners escaping down the Flint River from the Andersonville prison. Escapees knew to seek out Dr. Chapman who assisted them in making their way to the Union blockade.

Dr. Chapman spent many uneasy nights sleeping under the pews at the Trinity Episcopal Church, hiding from Confederate soldiers. The fact that he was a skilled physician and a surgeon saved his life more than once. Doctors like Chapman were few. Dr. Chapman cherished life over his Northern sympathies, and it made no difference to him whether that life was Yankee or Rebel.

Time dragged on, and with so little commerce, it was hard to keep busy. In the late afternoon, about four-thirty p.m., I stood up to stretch my legs, and out of the second floor window just down the street on a bench, I spotted Pearl. The zeal I felt that morning re-energized me. I returned to my desk, grabbed the flour sack, and headed down the stairs and out the French doors.

Pearl noticed me right away and gave me a smile unique to herself, a special smile only she possessed.

As I approached her, she stood and curtsied. "Good afternoon, Mr. Brandon. What is the news of the day, Mr. Brandon?"

"I'm afraid no news, Miss Pearl. Things have been rather quiet. You are looking very beautiful."

"Why thank you for saying so, Mr. Brandon. Miss Charity just finished getting me all cleaned up and ready for the evening. I've been helping her with the Orman laundry today. Did you enjoy your meal at Miss Caroline's?"

"Immensely," I replied.

"After you left, Miss Caroline and I laughed and laughed. I told her you seemed so flustered that you left without paying your bill. She didn't seem worried at all. I spent the rest of the evening helping Miss Caroline pick out the perfect dress for the church picnic. I don't think I'm spreading rumors when I tell you she seems very excited about the picnic."

Sitting beside Pearl on the bench, I let her know I was also eager.

"Miss Pearl I have something for you; will you be permitted to receive a small gift?"

46

Pearl's expression became one of jubilation. I had the feeling I might have overplayed the importance of this gift. "Oh, Mr. Brandon, you have a gift for me? What is it? What is it?"

"Now Miss Pearl, don't get overwrought. It is just a few items I have been saving, and rather than them gathering dust in a closet, I thought you might make use of them."

The expression Pearl gave me was one worthy of a castle, and all I had to offer was a flour sack with a mirror and a brush and a small bottle of perfume. I handed the gift to her. She held it for a moment, squeezing the items through the sack. Holding it up, she opened the top and let out a squeal.

"Oh, Mr. Brandon. Mr. Brandon! How wonderful. Are you sure these are really for me? I can't believe these are really for me."

"I hope you can make good use of these. They belonged to my mother." I stood up.

"Miss Pearl, I'm afraid I have to leave you now. I need to go back and lock up the Customs House. I'll see you later." I excused myself.

She held the mirror. "Thank you, Mr. Brandon. These are so wonderful."

Peering out the Customs House window, I watched Pearl as she stood, carefully taking inventory of every item, gently laying them in a row on the bench in front of her. She returned to each item, picked it up, and treated it as though it were a great treasure.

Pearl gazed into the mirror and gently brushed her hair. I watched as she removed the glass stopper from the perfume bottle. She dabbed a small amount behind her ears. Carefully replacing the stopper, Pearl put the bottle back on the bench. I cannot remember a time when I had been more anxious to present a gift, but to have that gift received so graciously put my spirits on a pedestal. Miss Pearl once again made my day special. It was now after six p.m., and I had preparations to make before my outing with Miss Caroline the next day.

\*\*\*

At thirty-nine years old, I was proficient in matters concerning commerce, banking, and export, none of which in any way prepared me for courting. The facts bore out that I had eaten one meal at her restaurant, a meal I ate alone. I based my entire mindset on information I extracted from a conversation with a seven-year-old child.

I was obsessing, unable to muster even a modicum of control. I went over the meal in my mind: she held my arm and led me to a table; she continually placed her hand on my shoulder to assess my well-being. I cannot fathom how in my mind I now justified holding Miss Caroline in such high esteem. How powerful was the feeling that carried me to her doorstep on Sunday morning. A relationship should have been against my better judgment with the threat of war so near.

As soon as I knocked, the door opened, and Miss Caroline presented herself in all her finery. My fears dried into dust and blew away. Once again, I found myself lost, gazing into those hypnotic, hazel-green eyes—where everything made sense. She moved to my side and took my arm.

"Why, Michael, you are the dashing gentleman today." Growing up, people called me Brandon after my father. It was my parents, Hatch, and Jacob called me Michael. I liked her calling me Michael, but tonight she could have called me mullet face, and I would not have noticed.

Tripping over my tongue, my response was a garbled word, followed by, "beautiful."

I must have gotten my point across because she responded with, "Why, thank you; shall we proceed?" I walked down the street with Miss Caroline on my arm, feeling like a king.

The last person I wanted to see when I entered the churchyard was Hatch Wefing. Hatch was one of my best friends, but just as I found myself inflicted with shyness, Hatch was overwhelmingly charismatic. Hatch knew everybody in town and everything about everybody, and he'd heard rumors about Miss Caroline and myself.

He smiled, then approached like a buzzard, looking at me as if I were a ripe carcass.

Then he ignored me and turned his attention to Caroline. "Miss Caroline, I declare you are a vision of loveliness although I see you have

48

a rather large canker protruding from your arm. No need to fear, for I am sure Dr. Chapman could nip that right off. Would you like me to go find the doctor?"

"No, no, that won't be necessary. Mr. Brandon kindly offered to escort me this Sunday," Caroline said.

I glared at Hatch, clinching my lips as a signal for him to be still. Hatch took a long look at me and continued. "Oh, well, I'll be. That is Mr. Brandon. Why, I am surprised at you, Miss Caroline; have you been gambling? Did you lose a wager? Do you now find yourself forced to take this old, tough piece of gristle to the church picnic? You do know he is so gristly that when he was young not even a 'gator would eat him."

"Well, I am no 'gator if that is what you are implying Mr. Wefing. I find Mr. Brandon most charming." She clutched my arm, looked up at me and smiled, and we continued on our way.

I smirked at Hatch as we moved away. Hatch was grinning ear to ear. As we entered the Trinity foyer, the Vicar made it a point to let me know that he was joyful I rediscovered the path leading to the church and looked forward to my being a Sunday regular as my father had been before me. Using work as an excuse, I allowed church to become seasonal, like cotton. The truth is I avoided attending alone, feeling much like a third wheel.

The service was under way by eight-thirty a.m. and contained within its context the responsibility of a soldier and a message of compassion and forgiveness of our enemies. Occasionally, the pipe organ would bring the congregation to their feet for a hymn. I had missed the sound of that organ. When it bellowed, you could hear it all the way to the bay. The bass pipes made the air vibrate, sending the hymn clear to one's soul. Our Vicar used the organ as a tool to keep the congregation alert.

The women of the church kept an elbow at the ready, rousing the men folk to their feet for each hymn. In anticipation of the day, I had not slept well, and although I found myself yawning under my breath, I would not require an elbow. Miss Caroline sat at my side. Her perfume, smelling of vanilla, added a wonderful distraction when the sermon began to drone.

Hatch, with one of his lady admirers, sat just across the aisle, occasionally glancing over his shoulder, giving me a look of approval with a nod and a smile. The service ended at twelve thirty p.m., and the congregation filed down the center aisle to visit with the Vicar.

Across the street, City Square had tables set ready for the older congregation; blankets were spread on the ground by others. I began to worry the picnic was a potluck, and it had not occurred to me to prepare anything for the event. I surveyed the area in a panic, looking for an escape, when Caroline said, "Here we are."

She sat down on the edge of a blanket already covered with the accoutrements needed for the event. How did she pull this off? It occurred to me that she had an accomplice. Scanning the area, I spotted a small, very well-dressed girl on a bench at the front of the church—Pearl.

Pearl had been listening to the sermon from the bench and had made all the preparations before the service ended. Miss Caroline saw me smiling at Pearl. Looking back at Caroline, I asked if it would be all right for Pearl to join us. I had been too long without a family; with Pearl and Caroline, I recalled the days of my youth and picnics with my parents. It took an event like this to make me realize how much I had taken family for granted.

God had designed this day just for me. Caroline and I talked all afternoon, getting to know each other, interrupted only by the occasional friend or neighbor who stopped by to chat and wish us well.

Pearl was in her heaven with so many people to talk to. Miss Sadie and her mother Miss Annie attended. Miss Sadie was being an instigator, encouraging conversations of gossip with Pearl just to irritate Miss Annie. Miss Charity came too and attended to the needs of the Orman family.

Hatch, who in fact was like a large child, ignored his companion and spent most of his time with his parents or told stories to the children. I could tell by the expressions on faces of the children that a lot of mothers and fathers would look under beds tonight to check for the menacing creatures living in Hatch's mind.

The picnic ended with a cleanup and a most wonderful hug from Pearl. I escorted Caroline home, carrying a basket that contained the last remnants of the picnic. It is not polite to air one's love life in public, so I simply record that the evening ended with a long hug and a legendary kiss.

***

The mail arrived by steamer the next morning. I knew that in Washington my having been born in the South did not bode well. The letter I received was to inform me that the running of the Port of Apalachicola now, and until further notice, would fall under the control of Union military command. I thought this a bold statement to make considering the apparent absence of a Union presence. My position was suspended until resolution of the current conflict.

I sat for a moment, collecting my thoughts. I mentally thanked my father and mother who, in their thrift, left me with the resources I would need to survive the conflict. I packed my possessions, notified my assistants of the contents of the letter, and released them from service. At one o'clock, I locked the door and walked away.

The streets that should be bustling with business now were sparsely occupied. The cotton warehouses sat locked. In past years, only during a drought could the river decide the fate of the cotton season.

In the evening, Caroline's business was no better than mine. I insisted she lock up and walk with me to the Fuller Hotel. The food at the Fuller was famous up and down the coastline and rated as the best. Fuller Hotel was owned by businessman, Anson Hancock. Mr. Hancock had extensive land holdings and in 1860 was one of eleven men who controlled sixty percent of the slaves in Franklin County, owning twenty-two. But everyone in Apalachicola knew the success of the Fuller Hotel was due to the efforts of Spartan Jenkins along with William Fuller and his wife Mary. It was because of Mary's popularity as a cook that the hotel was known as the Fuller. To say the least this was a strange partnership, but if anything could overcome race, it was profit in commerce.

Old man Jenkins, Spartan's father, was a successful businessman and owner of several properties with vested interests in more than one local business. Some viewed his black wife as his only liability. When old man Jenkins died, he left his mulatto son Spartan well provided for, and all things considered, Spartan had done an admirable job of following in his father footsteps to maintain the family's business interests.

William Fuller was a free black from Baltimore, Maryland, and his wife, Mary Adeline, was a former slave from a plantation in Jackson County, Florida. I never truly understood the connection between Spartan and the Fullers that led to their partnership. I suspect that Spartan brought him in on the deal, and William fell in love with the slave cook, Mary, that Anson purchased from a Jackson County plantation. What I can tell you for sure was it was common knowledge in Apalachicola that the Fuller Hotel was in truth a black owned hotel, and Anson Hancock was more than happy to turn a blind eye to the daily operations, finding himself content to sit back and count his money. It wouldn't be until 1889, after the death of Anson, his wife Susan, and their son Nathaniel, that it would officially be sold to Spartan and the Fullers.

During these difficult times, the Fuller Hotel was surviving against all odds, due to its high standards, renowned menu, and the fact that they catered to whites.

Even here at the Fuller, you could tell the upcoming war was threatening. You could see it on faces and hear it in voices. Despite the hardships, the meal was exceptional, and Caroline's company took my mind off my own troubles. Eventually, I revealed the content of the letter and told her that although my prospects were greatly diminished, she had no need to worry. No matter what the war had in store for us, I would be there for her.

After leaving the restaurant, we sat on the porch of the hotel, talking and laughing until dark. The town appeared empty as we stepped onto the street. I tried to lead Caroline toward the Florida House, but she caught my arm and turned me toward my home. I could say we were strong and talked all night, but in truth, when we rose in the morning, in

God's eyes, we were wed in the flesh. She was gone in the morning before I awoke. She had traveled back to the Florida House.

As the year dragged on, Caroline and I became inseparable. I felt I had no right to this much joy when my friends and neighbors faced such peril. I considered my friends often in an attempt to maintain a perspective on the war.

The battles of the war up to now were minor skirmishes, each side testing the strength and resolve of the other. On August 7, 1861, word reached us that matters had changed on July 21 at a town in Virginia called Manassas. Over two thousand Confederate soldiers were missing, injured, or dead. I could not understand how people could celebrate this battle as a victory.

The commitment of both North and South now solidified, and it was apparent that a resolution would not be found in diplomacy but rather in a long and costly war. I could not wrap my mind around the staggering number of dead and injured at the battle in Manassas. Nor could I have known that by the end of 1864, these numbers would pale in comparison to those in the battles to come.

At the time, I found some comfort in knowing Jacob had traveled to Tennessee. I could not have foreseen that in Tennessee he now faced the worst of the fray.

Caroline would try to ease the guilt I felt for not being there with my friends, but she made no apologies and never concealed her joy that I was absent from the terrifying events. It was unspoken, but we both knew I would make a poor soldier. Whereas I would hesitate and consider the humanity, forfeiting my life, others would instinctively strike out without hesitation. This chasm in our nature is what separated Jacob and me.

Hatch ran steamers nonstop, picking up armaments from the steel works and clothing from the mill in Columbus, Georgia. He stopped by for a brief visit to fuel before the last leg of the journey to take his cargo to supply troops mustered in Pensacola. He came to the Florida House and shared a meal, telling us all the happenings upriver and along the coastline. More than once, we owed our lives to Hatch, who brought us advanced warning and news, and, on many occasions, supplies to help sustain us through the lean times.

Although small in comparison to the deeds of Jacob and Hatch, the least I could do was to maintain their homes and keep close watch on the families they left behind.

*\*\*\**

On Tuesday, April 16, 1861, I decided not to remain idle due to the suspension of my employ. The first stop was the docks, where I purchased eight mullet and a half bag of oysters. My first visit was to Jacob's mother Jenny, who, like everyone else, was feeling the hardships of these difficult times. She feared for her son. When she cried, I struggled to hold back my own tears. I tried to comfort her by telling her she raised a resourceful son who could take care of himself. I held her hand and assured her that he was being cautious and looking forward to a home-coming.

God forgive me for my lies; my fears shadowed her own. I left her a couple of mullet and a few oysters for a meal. She hugged me, telling me how blessed she was that her son had such good friends. Moving on to Hatch's parents, I repeated the gesture. I followed the same path through town three to four days a week during the course of the war. It was a responsibility I willingly embraced: a duty to my friends. When I began, my intent was pure, but because the deed seemed to ease my conscience, I wondered if on some level my motive was selfish. I have never been able to reconcile that any task I might perform here could in any way compensate for my failure to serve active duty during the war. I struggled to quell my feelings of insecurity and continued my service in honor of my absent friends.

By noon, three steamers arrived from Columbus carrying troops and supplies. The town, once again, came to life. I passed Caroline's dining room, which for the first time in weeks was hiring additional help to serve food. Pearl waved as she rushed from table to table, even serving plates to men sitting on the steps and the ground.

Not wanting to burden Caroline with an additional presence, I continued on my way. I felt concern for Pearl whose wave seemed reserved and her eyes sad. I passed by the Customs House and felt empty. Having always worked, I felt useless as well.

Walking on to Market Street, I gazed through the windows of the shops. At the local Lombard Pawnshop, my heart skipped a beat. Through the window, I saw my mother's comb, brush, and mirror. A bell attached to the door rang as I entered and the pawnbroker quickly approached.

I pointed to the items in the window.

"The grooming set just arrived," he informed me.

When I questioned who had brought them, he claimed his assistant purchased the merchandise, and he could not reveal the seller. We brokered a deal, and I grudgingly purchased the set. I would now need to have a sit-down with Pearl. He carried the grooming set behind the counter to wrap it in paper and twine. Noticing cases of jewelry, my mind turned to Caroline. Of all the pieces displayed in the case, one necklace stood out. When the shop owner returned, I asked to view the necklace.

The broker unlocked the case, and through glass, I identified the necklace from the others on display. Removing it from the case, he handed it across the counter, telling me, "Excellent choice, sir; one of my finest."

It was a small, carved shell, floral cameo pendant with sapphires, hung from a silver chain. I turned it over, and in a vision, I was back in Saint Joseph once again. I felt my mother's cold body as I carried her from the burial pit. The necklace was engraved "C.G.K." Cora Grace Kohler.

My blood began to pound in my head, and I felt myself losing focus. I gripped the counter to find support until I could recover. I could not conceive of my mother and father's bodies being robbed, then thrown like so much rubbish into a pit.

My reaction disturbed the broker, and his hand dropped below the case. Without seeing, I knew he now gripped a revolver.

He tried to calm me. "To be honest, this piece has been here for years. You're the first to take notice. Tell you what, keep it as a part of the grooming set. Would you find that agreeable?"

Nervously, he handed the package across the counter, keeping his other hand firmly planted under the case. I gripped the necklace in my hand, taking the parcel in the other. How quickly my day had turned bitter. For the next few hours, I walked blindly through the streets.

The days were long this time of year and the sun still over an hour from setting. At eight p.m., I was in sight of Caroline's. As I approached, out of the corner of my eye, I spotted Pearl sitting on a keg in an alley. She saw me but made no effort to rise and welcome me. She was noticeably disturbed. She wrung a handkerchief in her hands.

Any anger I could have felt turned to concern. I had never seen Pearl so distraught. Sitting down on a crate beside her, I stroked the back of her head. "Pearl, sweetheart, what's wrong?"

"Oh, Mr. Brandon, I have done something so terrible. I just know when you find out, you won't like me anymore."

I tried to ease her distress. "Pearl, I want you to calm down, and let me be the judge of that. Now tell me what happened."

She unclasped her hand and along with the handkerchief, she held the small bottle of perfume I had given her.

"It's all I got left of your wonderful gift. I ran back to show Miss Charity, and she said I was truly blessed to have a good friend like you, but I sinned and took too much pride. I always leave my treasures in a wardrobe at Miss Charity's, but I loved your gift so much I wanted to look at it over and over again, and that's my sin. I didn't hide it away. My sin is my pride and my vanity. I was lookin' in my mirror, brushin' my hair when my papa burst through door. He'd been taking the medicine.

"When he saw them gifts, he said, 'You steal them girl? Ugly little whelp like you don't need nor deserve no fancy brush.' He pulled them away from me, and I haven't seen them since.

"I'm so sorry, Mr. Brandon, I hope you can forgive me 'cause no gift in the world is as special to me as you. I just can't bear losin' you."

Pearl climbed off the keg and hugged me as she cried bitterly. I stroked her hair, assuring her everything was going to be all right. When she calmed herself, I picked her up and sat her back on the keg.

"Pearl, I will always and forever be your friend. Nothing can change that. It is like the sun always rising. You can count on that. As for your feeling like you have sinned…." I then put the paper parcel on her lap.

"I'm going over to visit Miss Caroline. When I leave, I want you to open this package, and when you've had time to think about it and calm down, I want you to come over and visit with me and Miss Caroline. God would not allow a gift like this to a little girl who was a sinner."

I walked out of the alley. Caroline, who had been listening from the street, came up and gripped my arm. She raised her hand to my face and stroked my cheek.

"Oh, Mr. Brandon, you are such a sweet man."

We walked across the street to the Florida House and sat on the porch. Caroline looked at me as though I had just saved the town. I struggled to stay in the moment, but I found myself brooding on the events of the afternoon. The abhorrence I felt for Pearl's father burned in me and consumed all my better judgments. Caroline could tell I was present but no longer there.

"What are you thinking right now?" She reached across the table and took my hands.

I was full of rage and out of control. The words spewed from my mouth: "Her father, that bastard!"

Just then, Pearl exited the alley and headed our way, with a smile to lift the spirits.

"Caroline, I'm sorry. I am so sorry. I didn't mean to sound so cruel," I told her.

"It's all right; you're fine now," she said. As Pearl approached, Caroline whispered, "I've been contemplating the bastard too."

Pearl climbed onto Caroline's lap and showed her the treasures she held in the parcel. She took them out, one at a time, and placed them on the porch.

Then it occurred to me, and I announced, "Pie! It's too bad we don't have any pie. Wouldn't that be a fabulous way to end the evening?"

Pearl and Caroline both smiled and rose to their feet. "Pearl, what do you think? Could we find some pie for Mr. Brandon?"

Pearl giggled. "I'm not sure, but I think I saw some sweet potato pies in the kitchen safe."

Where I was blunt and awkward, Caroline was a master of conversation. As we enjoyed the pie, Caroline was able to learn Pearl's immediate situation. Her father was gone, and Pearl was staying with Miss Charity. We sent Pearl on her way, safe and content. I stood with Caroline on the porch as Pearl disappeared around the corner.

Turning to Caroline, I presented her with the cameo, placing it around her neck. "This belonged to my mother. I know she would want you to have it."

*** 

I was up early the next morning, sitting on the porch of the Florida House. It appeared as though I had just arrived and wanted breakfast.

Two weeks later, Caroline and I were both heart-broken when we discovered Pearl and her father had left. Because they were transient and were never seen together, Pearl's illusive father remained unknown to us.

Caroline visited and spoke with Miss Charity at her shack. They consoled each other, both distressed over Pearl's circumstance. Not even Miss Charity could identify the face of Pearl's father. She knew from a letter Pearl possessed he was Belgian, and his name was Guillaume Gauthier Verheist.

"There be slaves live here from the old times. These slaves they do not know this man, but they know of his father and his grandfather 'cause they be slavers of the worst kind. I don't believe that apple fall far from that tree 'cause he don't even share his name with Miss Pearl. She carries her mama's name," Miss Charity said.

Miss Charity told Caroline that Pearl's father wanted nothing to do with her and tolerated her because of an oath forced on him by her mother.

Miss Charity let Pearl keep what she called her treasures and dresses at her shack in a large wardrobe.

Miss Charity was one of thirty-five slaves who belonged to Mr. Thomas Orman. She lived in the slave shack behind the Orman house. Caroline learned that Charity had borne four children—her master Mr. Thomas believed they were all his children. She confessed she had been newly pregnant, showing no signs, with her eldest son when she was purchased by Thomas Orman. He assumed the boy was his, and she saw no benefit in his knowing any different.

Orman was surprised when Charity produced enough money to buy her son's freedom. That son, Matthew, was a free black minister. Her second boy, Mark, died of the fever at the age two. Her third son, Luke, was sold when he was six years old, and she had not heard from him since. Her baby boy, Milton, traveled with Thomas Orman's white son, William, in the war.

Miss Charity told Caroline that she first saw Pearl when she was about four years old; she was sitting on a bench by the docks.

Pearl had been instructed, perhaps threatened, by her father to wait until he finished work. Charity befriended Pearl, and during the day, she kept her close and taught her how to take care of herself. Pearl gave Miss Charity a hand-full of letters and asked her to read them, hoping they would reveal more about her mother.

Other than entering the wardrobe to care for Pearl's dresses, Charity honored Pearl's privacy, but today she took a box from the top shelf, removed a letter, and handed it to Caroline.

Caroline told me later that the letter addressed to Pearl was from her mother. Caroline explained the letter, "brought tears from us both as I read it aloud." Even facing death, Pearl's mother unquestionably loved her daughter. The necklace Pearl wore around her neck was a reminder of her mother's love.

As Caroline read the letter, Charity moved across the room and removed an envelope from a small cabinet. "This be a letter I hid from the ones Miss Pearl brought me. God forgive me, but I don't think she need know about this letter. I've often thought about burnin' it in the fire."

This letter was from Pearl's mother to her father, and it revealed that Pearl's mother was, in fact, a gypsy. The letter spoke to him about her family in New Orleans, and because she was now dying, he was responsible for their child's well-being. The letter addressed his cruel ways and her confession of her practice of the dark African art of Hoodoo. The letter spoke of spells, curses, and the deal she made with the dead to protect her daughter from his brutality. Strange signs and symbols filled the margins of the paper.

She made it clear there was no place on earth he could hide from the curse she placed on him if death were to befall her precious daughter.

"Miss Caroline, let it be known I don't believe in Hoodoo and Voodoo. What is important is her Papa do, and as long as he do, he'll not lift a hand to hurt our girl. He say things to Pearl to hurt and try gettin' in her mind, but you know Pearl, her spirit like a shield to protect her from the words. I don't believe we need tarry on the fate of Miss Pearl. I know down deep in my soul that this child has been special blessed by God himself.

"I know things about this child that someday, when it come into the light, will place her among the saints in heaven. Now you go on, and you and Mr. Brandon try not to fret. You a lucky woman to have been courted by Mr. Brandon 'cause Miss Pearl have blessed Mr. Brandon, and she have blessed you and the upcoming union."

Caroline said the breath caught in her throat as Charity spoke on. "Tell Mr. Brandon someday I am lookin' forward to speakin' to him eye to eye about a few things he need to know about Pearl."

\*\*\*

While Caroline and Charity spoke, I had returned to my house. Once again, I sat on the floor in front of the chest containing the effects of my mother and father. I had a mission and knew precisely why I searched. Soon after, in the palm of my hand, I held my mother's wedding rings. Knowing she was dying, she had removed the rings and placed them in a small box on her dresser. I placed them in the watch pocket of my trousers and returned to the Florida House.

Caroline arrived soon after and began to talk of the unusual visit to Charity. She ended quoting the words of Charity, "She have blessed you and the upcoming union." I, like Caroline, now found the breath halted in my throat. I reached into my watch pocket and revealed the rings.

"Caroline, precious Caroline, would you consent to be my wife?" Caroline sat speechless—I caught her completely off guard.

She looked at me and simply said, "Yes." These were strange times and uncanny forces seemed to be at work. I felt it best not to face this future alone.

We celebrated that night at the Fuller Hotel with a good meal and a bottle of champagne. We decided to put the ceremony on hold until Pearl returned and could be a part of the celebration. This was also a way to reassure ourselves of her return.

*"The Stars and Bars" First National Flag of the Confederacy*

# Chapter VI

## Life under Siege

Since June 1861, the only threat on our shore was the occasional appearance of the USS Montgomery patrolling the coastline. On December 1, 1861, Hatch reported that down the Atlantic coastline, Confederate ports were under siege. The Union Navy had been making improvements and was now effectively blockading Southern ports. The Confederacy was responding with smaller, faster ships that could outmaneuver the larger Union vessels. Hatch believed the Gulf Coast would be next and advised us to collect and ration our supplies.

Caroline and I were happy to report to Hatch that we had been laying in a good supply of smoked and salted meats along with barrels of grain, salt, sugar, molasses, dried beans, peas, Tupelo honey, peanuts, and flour. I told him I even had two barrels of his favorite smoked mullet stored upstairs at my Cedar Street house, the house I moved from St. Joseph and now called my home.

Hatch had been adding to our stocks with several crates of these new canned goods, including condensed milk and potted meats. The milk was flavorsome enough, but up until this point, we had not sampled the potted meats.

The steamboats once carrying cotton were commandeered by the Confederacy to carry troops and supplies and make regular runs between Pensacola, New Orleans, and Columbus, Georgia. The boarding houses, hotels, and restaurants of Apalachicola were now housing and feeding the officers and soldiers of the Confederacy who were left behind to oversee movement of supplies along the Gulf Coast.

Hatch returned on December 18, 1861, with disturbing news. The USS Hatteras was now lying just off St. Vincent Island near the site of the dismantled battery. The few Confederate soldiers who remained on the islands reported that a small complement of Union soldiers had visited the abandoned battery on St. Vincent Island and the lighthouse at

*Cape Saint George Lighthouse*

Cape St. George. Although the Confederates had earlier dismantled and removed the light, it was now from this high point that the Union soldiers observed the town. Shortly after the Union returned to their ship, the Confederates slipped in and burned the interior staircase, leaving a hollow shell.

To ease the fear I now saw on Caroline's face, I commented that they could not have seen much more than the hull of an uncompleted ship, a few fishing smacks, and an occasional steamer.

"Caroline, I don't want you to worry. Nothing here poses a threat to the Union Navy. Chances are they will discover we are undefended and leave us be."

The last remnants of the Confederate forces abandoned us the week of March 16, 1862. They disappeared into the interior and along the coastline. We realized we were alone and at the mercy of the Union ships. Other than a couple of dozen white families of mostly women and children, a few Italian and Greek oystermen, and a handful of slaves, by the week of March 23, 1862, the town had been abandoned.

The Union Navy would have been lucky to find four-hundred souls remaining in the entire area. The very makeup of our town had placed us in a precarious position. It was unfortunate that the greatest threat we now faced was from our own compatriots. Many of the oystermen who remained behind refused service in the Confederate forces. Some of the men remaining in town were in fact Northern sympathizers who refused to serve. These men looked to the Union blockade for protection of their families and property.

Men of Confederate sympathies that were left behind, unable to serve, banded together and considered the other men as "Southern, damn Yankees." Those citizens who remained in town, no matter their sympathies, were under the same threat from the so-called Confederates. Threats of incineration and malice hung like a storm cloud over the town. Trust was waning, rumors abounded, and suspicion ran rampant.

In the early morning of Monday, March 24, 1862, we realized our greatest fear. Two boats, a cutter and a whaler, launched from the *USS Mercedita*. They carried on board a full complement of heavily armed troops and were rowing toward our town.

From sheltered positions, we watched as the boats approached. The whaleboat led the cutter by five-hundred yards, searching the shoreline for signs of aggression. The larger cutter lay waiting, ready to come to the aid of the smaller boat. Both boats approached under a flag of truce. Eventually, both boats came within one-hundred yards of the lower wharf and anchored. The oars were kept up, as a signal that the boat commander wished to communicate with Apalachicola leaders.

One half-hour passed, and no one from the town came forward. The commander of the Union expedition raised anchor and proceeded toward the lower wharf. I was relieved when I saw Mayor Anson Hancock, and three of our city leaders, City Clerk Sam Benezet, Mr. Richard Gibbs Porter, and John Miller, all prominent merchants, filing onto the dock.

The ranking Union officer introduced himself as Lieutenant Trevett Abbot of the *Mercedita* and reported the object of his mission. Mr. Hancock informed Lt. Abbott that by order of the Confederate government the local Confederate command had removed troops, arms, and ammunition the previous week, and he could not speak to their current disposition. He informed Lieutenant Abbott that all inhabitants except for themselves and a few women and children had left.

"We, the few, have remained behind to protect our own properties from incineration threatened from onshore," he said.

Hancock also informed Lt. Abbott the city leaders and the women and children gathered had no authority to represent the new Confederate government.

A perceptive man, Lieutenant Abbott noticed that except for these four leaders, all other citizens watching stayed back a considerable distance. He also noted their nervous demeanor, concluding that some of these men were under threat from Confederate ruffians, so-called Confederates, which were now standing in the shadows, watching the proceedings.

He appeared convinced that the same leaders he spoke with were possibly rank secessionists and that through them he would never be able to ascertain the true sentiments of the town. Lt. Abbott wisely decided not to raise the Union flag or insist that the citizens take the loyalty oath.

He realized that the citizens of Apalachicola were under the threat of death if caught collaborating with the enemy. He concluded the interview and returned to his ship. Had I known Lieutenant Abbott in a different circumstance, I could have viewed him as a friend. The citizens of Apalachicola breathed a sigh of relief as he rowed away.

On April 3, 1862, Lieutenant in Command A. J. Drake, of the US gunboat *Sagamore,* launched eight armed boats and captured without resistance the city of Apalachicola, along with all vessels in the vicinity. This was a blow to Southern pride, but I viewed it as a mixed blessing. At least now, we no longer had to live with the uncertainty of whether the Federals or the Confederates were in charge of our town.

The people remaining in Apalachicola, mostly women and children, crowded the wharves to watch the eight, heavily-armed boats, landing on our shore.

They earlier had been convinced that the Yankee forces were ruthless Hessians bent on burning, pillaging, and destroying. Because of Lieutenant Abbott, they stood without any fear of mistreatment and seemed to believe that the Yankees might possess a degree of humanity and discipline.

The Yankees once again returned to their ships under command to blockade the port, not occupy the town. Much to our disdain, they returned many times to commandeer supplies and collect intelligence, but the town, for now, did not face the utter destruction previously predicted.

Steamers had disappeared from our river, replaced by small, fast boats belonging to the blockade runners. I believed the blockade runners to be the enemy of both sides.

Privateers and pirates ran cargo past the blockade up the river and, driven by greed, sold the cargo at excessive prices, profiting on the backs of a devastated people. Whenever the boats made it past the blockade, the town would fall under suspicion, and the Union troops would come ashore, searching for answers.

*Union Blockaders fire on Blockade Runner, Apalachicola Bay.*
Image RC05589, ***Harper's Weekly, 1864***

By August, 1862, the Union blockaders became very efficient, and under the objections of local leaders, the Confederate army blockaded the last channel that supplied provisions from the North. Many in the town began to suffer from malnutrition.

Our citizens felt betrayed by the Confederate commanders' decision to cut our supply line. They looked to the Union blockaders, and the Union responded. Once again Union boats returned to town and in tow brought several boats they had captured which were attempting to run the blockade. The boats presented to the townspeople were to be used to harvest seafood to feed the town.

The gift of the boats came with a warning. If found to be collecting more food than was necessary, the Union would fire on the boats. The health of the town soon improved with the variety of seafood. Caroline and I shared what we had to maintain the families of our friends who served in the war. We made frequent trips to Trinity church, bringing food and preparing meals for those less fortunate. The less fortunate also included slaves left behind. One of the slaves was a man named Stillman Smith.

Stillman Smith was taller than average and of a slender build. He was of a medium black color and could have been mistaken for mulatto. Although considered illiterate, he was surprisingly articulate. Stillman was a jack-of-all-trades with a working knowledge of carpentry, woodworking, and blacksmithing. A slave with Stillman's talents would have commanded a high price.

He presented himself as a self-ordained free man, liberated from a plantation in South Carolina. His deceased master had made the mistake of firing on a company of Union soldiers and was shot himself.

Stillman's skills were revealed to the Vicar. Because he considered himself a man of principle, he could not in good conscience accept food as charity, so he worked odd jobs around the church to pay for his keep. I spoke with him and instantly liked the man.

I was born and raised in the South, but up until this point, I had not taken the time or effort to communicate with members of the slave community. Fascinated and intrigued by Stillman Smith, I needed to examine him more closely. A question arose in my mind: is it possible I had been misinformed about slaves? It occurred to me that if the rumors of the Yankees (comparing them to Hessians) were propaganda, perhaps slaves were more than mere livestock.

My father left me with the financial resources to survive this war, but I was finding myself overwhelmed with the work required to maintain all of the properties I now held in trust for my friends. I struck a deal with Stillman, hiring him to help me. The next morning, he greeted me as I left the house, eager to begin his new job.

I made my rounds, introducing Stillman as my employee, a skilled artisan who would be making needed repairs and improvements. Our last stop was the Florida House.

Caroline saw us coming and greeted us at the steps. She immediately extended her hand, and Stillman responded by taking it.

"It is a pleasure to meet you, Mr. Smith. I look forward to your helping out. Perhaps with you on the job, I might see a little more of Mr. Brandon," said Caroline.

"The pleasure is mine. I'll work hard to make sure Mr. Brandon's able to visit you more often," Stillman said.

Caroline never ceased to amaze me. By all appearances, she was color blind. Extending her hand to a black man was unacceptable in Apalachicola society, but because it was Stillman, I hardly took notice.

Hiring Stillman Smith was a good decision. He was a remarkable artisan, shoring up windows, digging weeds from yards and vegetable gardens, completing jobs faster than I could create them. He often took the initiative.

Many times, I would hear Stillman say, "You can take that off your list, Mr. Brandon. I already done fixed that." It was not long before Stillman's mental list was longer than the one I had written on paper. Most days, I would merely send Stillman on his way, telling him to use his own judgment and fix whatever needed fixing.

On larger jobs, like repairing leaky roofs, Stillman and I worked together, but because he had the skills, I would end up assisting and learning from him. My upbringing was telling me this thinking was wrong, but my mind and my heart told me that Stillman Smith, although black, was as much a man as I.

I was beginning to see the bridge that separated white and slave and was trying to understand the powerful society of oppression that had created it. The lies we were taught were created to maintain the status quo. Stillman never shirked his responsibility. He was a man of pride and honor, and after a short time, he had earned my trust.

Caroline and I were now able to spend more time together. We walked for miles, talking and making plans for the future. Other times, we would sit silent and lament the loss of Pearl.

# Chapter VII

# Turpentine

In the night of Sunday, December 7, 1862, at eleven thirty p.m. there was a knock on my door. I had rehearsed this scenario in my mind. Reaching for my father's saber and a revolver, I quietly stumbled down the stairs.

I laid the revolver on the small table I had strategically placed by the door. Holding the saber under my arm, I lit a candle. I was ready but quickly discovered I did not have enough hands to hold a pistol, candle, saber and unlock the door. I propped the saber against the table. Holding the candle in one hand, I unlocked the door with the other. The saber precariously balanced on the table, slipped, and fell to the floor, creating quite a racket. I pushed the saber out of the way with my foot, cutting my big toe as the door opened.

I am not sure, but I may have said a curse under my breath. The candle light revealed Hatch Wefing grinning from ear to ear. "Are you up for company?"

I was overjoyed to see my friend. I stepped toward him, threw my arms out, and embraced him. The candle blew out, but it didn't matter.

I proclaimed, "My God, man, it is good to see you. Come in, come in." I hugged him and patted his shoulders.

I made my way back into the house, leaning on Hatch, limping with my bad leg, and walking on the heel of my foot with the other to keep from bleeding on the floor. By that time, Caroline came down the stairs with a lamp, illuminating the room.

"What is going on down here?"

"It's Hatch, come for a visit," I replied, sounding giddy.

Hatch watched Caroline coming down the stairs. He chuckled and whispered, "You old dog."

Stillman, who was staying at the old home place on Laurel, heard the commotion, saw the candle go out, and came running with an ax in hand. I swear when Stillman burst into that room swinging that ax, I truly believe it may have taken a year off Hatch's life.

\*\*\*

After we all calmed down, Caroline patched up my toe and put on the kettle. She removed a chocolate cake from the kitchen safe, and we sat down for a grand visit.

August was the last time we heard from Hatch, and I feared him dead or captured.

Hatch extended his hand across the table. "Hatch Wefing."

Taking it, Stillman replied, "Stillman Smith."

"I want to thank you for helping take care of my family. My parents can't say enough about your good work," Hatch told Stillman.

"We all in this together, Mr. Hatch, and 'sides, Mr. Brandon, he pays me and give me a place to stay just for helpin' out."

Hatch then turned his attention to me. With both of us almost in tears, I spoke up.

"Hatch Wefing, don't you start up with me. I haven't done anything anyone else wouldn't have done, and it isn't even a small part of what you're doing, so just give me the news."

Hatch hesitated, placed his hand on my shoulder, and gave me a squeeze. "Michael, I am growing weary of these hostilities. We have been sold a bill of goods by a bunch of greedy politicians, the same politicians that got us all excited about a new country. A Confederate nation. Now I am just not sure.

"They're talkin' that Lincoln is going to free our slaves. Now, I don't like anybody telling me what I can and can't do, but you know as well as I do, we never owned a slave in our lives. The only people I know

71

who can afford slaves are the rich people, and they're the ones who stand the most to lose if Lincoln frees the slaves and the North wins. Fact is, they're the same people running this war."

"These plantation owners, these men of commerce, they've got their arms so far up the rears of Southern politicians that when they move their fingers, they run their mouths just like they were puppets. I'm finding myself not caring if they have to hire their labor if it saves our boys' lives. I'm starting to feel I might be helping to fight this war just so these rich, aristocratic bastards can keep their damn money."

"Amen," I replied.

"It's not as though most of them are fighting anyway. Lot of them bought their way out of service. They'd rather leave the fighting and dying up to the poor, white rebel boys who don't know any better and will follow them around like a herd of sheep to the slaughter.

"I tell you, there can't be any justification for a war when, after a single battle, ten thousand men have fallen. And it's not just one battle; these battles are getting hard to count. This is what is happening all over this country."

"Problem is armies are getting bigger, and the battles are getting bigger. If you think the battles were big this year, wait until next."

"I worry about Jacob," I told him.

"I hate to tell you, my friend, but Jacob is in the middle of it. Back in November, General Bragg started a new army up in Tennessee, and with what they are planning, it don't get any worse. I'm afraid if Jacob comes home, he might just be a shadow of the man we knew. The reason I stay in this war now is for the sake of my friends, until they come home safe.

"I blame you for all these foolish notions, rattling around in my head these days. When we were young, you always had to think too much, and you wanted to know why. Everything rubbed off on me, and I haven't had a good night's sleep since."

He put his arm around my shoulder. "I don't know these days if I'd be measured an abolitionist or not," he said.

"I do know I am sick and tired of our boys dying and the reasons for their deaths. I think if I'm an abolitionist, it's more than not that I'd be an abolitionist against the rich bastards who got us into trouble in the first place. I think, if we dragged them to the front lines and stuck guns in their hands, the war would be over damn quick."

We talked about the war and the old times into the early morning hours. As Hatch prepared to leave, he pulled me aside and asked a favor.

"I rented you two mules from the stable. Hitch your father's wagon and travel up to the old turpentine camp. You remember? Up across from Owl Creek, the place where Jacob's father died. Don't worry if you can't quite remember the way. Trust the mules; they know the way. Just get them on the Apalachee Trail and let them lead. Pick up a shipment, and carry it north to the Narrows. I will meet you there on the morning of January twelfth. Once I have the cargo, you will be free to return home."

I agreed to do as he requested.

"Michael, trust me when I say you need to make this journey. Tell no one."

Hatch left before sunrise to get back up-river to avoid a possible Union patrol boat.

\*\*\*

Following the old Apalachee Indian Trail, it was a half-day to the camp then a half-day on to the Narrows. I have always strived to be honest, which made it hard to tell Caroline I had to leave for a couple of days but could not reveal where or why. She would be safer not knowing. She eventually came around and grudgingly helped me prepare.

A little over a month later, I left in the early morning hours of Sunday, January 11, 1863. I never felt Caroline's love more than on that morning when I saw the worry in her face and heard the tremble in her voice. She repeatedly touched me and held on until our hands released as the wagon pulled away. I felt the pain of separation into the depths of my soul. I now understood why my father once said about my mother, "She is the air I breathe, and without her I will die."

I began my journey, traveling west of town on the old St. Joseph road. Finding myself once again in my father's wagon on this path filled my mind with the memories of long ago when I traveled this same road with a much different purpose.

About one mile west of town, I turned north and began the trek along the Apalachee Indian Trail. The cool weather of January had effectively dispatched the hordes of seasonal biting insects that otherwise would have made the journey intolerable.

I carried one of my father's loaded Colt Patersons on the seat beside me…not for the Yankees or highwaymen but because some of the locals had spotted a panther prowling near the slaughterhouse. I could not afford to lose a mule.

The day was pleasant, and my journey was under way. Except for the bumps in the road, I lowered my guard and relaxed. It was a long haul to the camp, and maybe rather than anticipate the worst, it would be better just to accept events as they happened.

Hatch had said something that started me thinking. Since I was a boy, I had been plagued with daydreams. Often, my father had to stir me from these waking dreams to set me back on a course of study. Hatch and Jacob would throw bits of rock and sticks at me when they caught me with a blind look in my eyes, staring into the distance. Although at the time, perceived as a notable lack of attention, these were times of great deliberations and contemplation as I searched for reason. Many times thoughts that began for understanding of some deep issues would end with Jacob, Hatch, and me fighting for survival, or treasure, against a Kraken from the deck of some doomed ship.

I was riding along, believing I finally had dominion over these waking dreams, when the mules reared: a family of wild hogs crossed the road in front of the wagon. Startled from my daydream, I almost fell off the wagon. Fully alert, I realized there might still be a boy somewhere inside who was not destined to change.

The mules led the way along the trail, sometimes north then east and west, occasionally even turning back south as they tracked their way along the forest trail. The river meandered to the east, making an occasional appearance and then again disappearing as the trail turned.

The road skirted a dwarf cypress swamp to the west. Its trees stood barren, needles having fallen in the cool breeze. Absent were gators and snakes, now finding haven from the cold by harboring in riverbank caverns or hollows formed in dead wood, on sunny days reappearing to take in the warmth of the sun.

Winter in the Florida Panhandle was just a date on a calendar compared to my childhood memories of Boston. In Apalachicola, some winters did not even realize a frost. Here a man might see his breath at six in the morning and shed his coat by ten. Even this time of year, some plants put on a show such as the coral plant whose red bean added color to the forest palette. Foliage of the forests and swamps remained mostly green, but a few yielded to yellow, amber, or deep reds, some showing the white down of fall as they released seeds into the wind. A few were blooming.

Fires often raged here, sometimes started by man in a feeble attempt to control, other times by God, with lightning to prune his forests. The people of this country understood that in the wake of fire, what appeared as hopeless devastation would find forgiveness by a land that in one brief season healed itself. Having sprung from fire for generations, some plants no longer reseeded without it. Men in the turpentine camps burned to get rid of the underbrush, eliminating many poisonous snakes and allowing better access to the trees where they harvested sap. Sometimes the timber workers burned, especially in boggy and swampish areas, to try to get rid of the ever-present mosquitoes, gnats, and other annoying bugs.

The mules, confident in their track, knew the way. After a few hours, I began to concentrate on a couple of smoked mullet and a piece of Caroline's sweet cornbread.

As I approached the camp, I could see activity in the pine forest and was surprised to see it still working.

Slaves and indentures with the tools of the trade scraped the trees to keep the sap flowing. Others dipped the sap from the box cuts in the base of the trees, pouring it into buckets. The buckets were poured into barrels on the back of a wagon that would carry the resin to the still. When the tree died, it was lumbered. I fell in behind one of the wagons and made my way into camp.

*Gathering Resin to Distill into Turpentine and Rosin.*

These camps were a law unto themselves and did not discriminate on the color of a slave. Indentured whites, many of them Irish, formed a large portion of the workforce. Some men came here starving, unable to find work any place else. Others were wanted men, running from the law or a military court martial. Mind the company's business, and you could survive; step out of line, and you might find yourself in a noose, hung by your friends.

In these remote areas, a slave master or camp owner could easily retrieve runaways. Blacks were an investment in capital and considered property. Black runaways received a whipping and were returned to work in chains. Punishment for a second offence was more severe and could result in death. Outside the camp, white indentures had more rights than black slaves but without the capital investment. The order was to shoot on sight for many white escapees, setting an example of what happens when you fail to pay the company store debt.

Men working the camps became used to the strong odor produced from cooking sap—the same scent that now burned my eyes and nose. The processed resin, now called rosin, was placed into barrels for the trip up-river to shipyards where it was mixed with hemp fiber and used to seal ship hulls. The turpentine collected during the process of cooking was used to make lamp oil, soap, ink, and lubricants. It was also an ingredient in medications and in salves to relieve respiratory ailments. The camp was just past the still. I was grateful it was also upwind.

*The Turpentine Still*

A young black boy, no more than nine, came running over, unhooked the rig, and started away with the mules.

"Mister, I take good care of the mules. Boss man over in the big house." He pointed toward a building serving as the office and company store. I entered the office and once again picked up the stench of the still. Out in the open, the breeze held the strong odor at bay, but the workers carried the scent on their clothes and in the pores of their skin. They seemed to sweat the very turpentine they distilled, and the odor quickly filled any space.

I was pleased to see the familiar face of James Hancock approaching with his hand extended.

"Brandon, it's good to see you. It's been a coon's age since we last met. Come on over and sit down. I've been expecting you. Hatch told me you were comin' for a shipment, and I am the fellow you need to see because I do the shipping. Although I have to say, it don't make no sense to me why Hatch would drag you all the way up here from Apalach in that little wagon for soap."

"Soap!" I exclaimed.

"Yes, I could just as easily send it like we usually do between the barrels of rosin, but Hatch insisted you needed to come up and take a load to the Narrows.

"Well, let me tell you James, I didn't know, and if I had, it might have saved me a long trip." James and I looked at each other thinking of Hatch and shaking our heads.

"As long as you're here, we might just as well make use of you. I'll have my men load your wagon. If you don't mind, would you walk down to the soap works and let 'em know you're here." He pointed out the window. "It's just down that trail a short piece."

I shook his hand again. "James, it's good to see you, and let me assure you, I'll have a few words for Captain Hatch when I see him at the Narrows."

James laughed, "Whatever you do, resist the temptation to shoot him. He comes in pretty handy at times. He's our best pilot."

I smiled then walked out the door and turned toward the trailhead.

# Chapter VIII

## Soap

I started down the trail when a voice yelled, "Hey, are you Kohler?"

"Yeah." I turned to see who had yelled. I was shocked to see the face of Jacob's father, but I knew it couldn't be him.

"Are you the Kohler that knows my nephew, Jacob Foley?" The man spoke with a strong Irish accent.

"Yes, that would be me. We grew up together."

"Good. I wanted to catch you to thank you for taking good care of Jacob's mother, Jenny, while he's away. It will mean a lot to him, knowing his sweet mother is being cared for."

"It is a privilege and my duty to a good friend," I told him as I shook his hand.

"Forgive me for not making formal introductions," he said. "I am Benjamin Foley, older brother of Jacob's poor departed father, Brian. I came over from Ireland a year ago, and with Brian's partners, I've been trying to make something of my brother's share of the land and business. Tell me, have you heard from Jacob lately?"

"My news of Jacob is old and informed me he was in the thick of things," I replied.

"I was afraid of that. Two days prior I was informed by one calling himself Mortimer Bates that he had been present on a battlefield where he witnessed Jacob fall, but being separated by battle, he could not relay the extent of Jacob's injury." With a discouraged brow, he shook his head.

I was stunned by the news. I shook my head in disbelief.

"I know Mortimer. He is a good man. I realize knowing is better, but in not knowing, there is still hope," I told him.

"It's a pleasure meeting you, and you are right; we will just have to continue hoping and praying." Choking back emotions, Benjamin extended his hand. "In the meantime, I best be off so when Jacob comes home, I can boast to him about how rich I've made us in his absence."

We parted ways, and I continued down the trail.

I was feeling about as low as a man could feel. As I approached the works, the smell of the pine tar soap brought back memories of all the unwanted and unnecessary baths I had taken in my youth. It reminded me of something Hatch used to say: "Hell, they make me wash my feet once a year whether I need to or not." The thought made me grin and took my mind off Jacob.

The soap works was a small building with part of the roof extending off one end. That part opened on three sides. In the shade of the roof, I could make out the silhouettes of a woman and a small boy standing beside a large salt kettle. As I approached, the boy turned and headed my way. He walked into the sun. He was wearing brown boots, light brown trousers, and a badly stained white shirt. His trousers were held up with a rope tied around his waist. His tan leather hat, well worn, flopped over his eyes.

As he drew near to me, he reached up and threw his hat to the ground. When I saw the face, I dropped, and Pearl leaped into my arms. My bad leg had me off balance, and we fell down. Flat on my back, we embraced. I grabbed her just above the waist and hoisted her into the air several times, letting out a yelp of pure celebration. She then straddled my chest, holding my face.

"Oh, Mr. Brandon, Mr. Hatch said you were comin'. I'm so glad you're here. I've been worried somethin' fierce about you and Miss Caroline. Now you're here, you can tell me all about ya." Then she stood up, "Everything's gonna be okay now."

We strolled hand in hand over to the soap works. Miss Charity gazed out at the commotion.

"Mr. Brandon, have you met Miss Charity?"

"I have not been formally introduced," I said. "Thank you for taking care of Pearl." I took Miss Charity by the hand.

"You're welcome," she replied.

By the time Pearl finished showing me around the camp and the building where she and Miss Charity stayed, the day was beginning to wane.

In a clearing, away from the smell of the soap works, a fire burned. Near the fire, Pearl had stacked an enormous pile of wood.

"I got us enough wood we can keep the fire burnin' and visit all night. Miss Charity says I can visit to my heart's content and watch the sun come up if I want to," said Pearl.

Using a metal shovel, Miss Charity gathered coals from the main fire. She carried the embers over to the cook fire and placed them under a black, wrought-iron pot. Three chains fastened to the iron frame suspended the cook pot just over the coals. Miss Charity spread a few coals on the ground near the simmering pot. She placed a Dutch oven on top of the coals then carefully covered the top of the oven with more coals.

"It's Miss Charity's stew," proclaimed Pearl, as she grabbed a rag to lift the lid from the simmering kettle.

"It's real good. I helped make it special for you. It's been simmerin' over that fire all day, and I been in charge of keepin' it stirred, so it don't burn." With what little she had, Pearl had gone out of her way to make my visit special. A small wooden table and three chairs sat near the larger fire. The table was set with some old silverware, worn cloth napkins, and wooden bowls. A small crock in the center of the table held plants Pearl had carefully collected.

With the sun now setting, Pearl and Charity served the meal, but only Pearl sat down at the table.

Pearl looked up at me and whispered, "You got to give Miss Charity permission to sit with us, and say it loud enough so people in ear-shot can hear ya. Otherwise she got to eat alone or with her own kind."

In a loud voice, I announced, "Miss Charity, I would like you to join us at the table?"

Pearl smiled and whispered, "Thank you, Mr. Brandon; that will keep Miss Charity from gettin' a beatin'."

The three of us enjoyed the stew with fresh baked Dutch oven biscuits, leaving plenty for seconds.

Although I was sure she had lots more to say, by eleven, Pearl faded off to sleep. I carried her back to the soap works and put her on her cot. Miss Charity covered her with an old blanket to keep off the night chill, and we returned to the fire.

I stood for a moment enjoying the crisp evening air. While she stoked the fire, I moved two of the chairs nearer.

"Mr. Brandon, would it be all right if I go on for a bit and tell you a few things you ought to know?"

I had been looking forward to this conversation for a long time. "Miss Charity, I wish you would."

"Your Miss Caroline probably done told you what I believe about Miss Pearl bein' a special child, but you doesn't know the half of it. Now I can't tell you everything 'cause it's up to Miss Pearl to do that in her own time and in her own way. But I will tell you, to lots of folk, Miss Pearl and her charms mean freedom."

"I know she's special," I said.

"Miss Pearl growed up hard. Her papa, he ain't no good, but he was kept at bay by a curse Pearl's mama put on him the night she was born. Miss Pearl, she a good daughter to him and try real hard to make him understand she love him. She try real hard to relieve the sickness that's in his mind."

Thinking about Pearl, Charity let out a little laugh before she could continue. "That girl is a fountain of never-endin' hope when it come to people. She got more cheeks to turn than all the peoples, in all the congregations, in all this world. Why, she's a fountain of never-ending words."

I thought to myself, both Pearl and Miss Charity.

"When I first met up with Pearl, she told me on one of her travels around town, waitin' for her papa to finish workin', she come upon a pile of fine looking charms. They was so perty she just knew they had to have been blessed. She collected up them charms and hid 'em away 'cause she afraid her papa might not let her keep 'em. She knew of lots of people who was bad off; maybe she could use some of them charms to help give them some comfort."

"Pearl also want to do what is right by God, so she go down and see the Vicar."

As Charity spoke, she reached into the pocket of her dress and withdrew a Meerschaum pipe, one of the finest I had ever seen. The bowl was carved with an exceptionally detailed face of a woman. She continued speaking as she packed the bowl of the pipe. "She tell the Vicar she want to help her friends by givin' out them charms but wanted to know what God might think about it."

"I know the Vicar, and he a good man, but he don't take Pearl serious 'cause she just a child. So he tell her to bring one of her charms down to the Trinity, and he gonna take a look at it and see what she might do with them charms to help her friends. Pearl come back a short time later, puttin' one of them charms in his hand. All of sudden, he felt the power that Pearl felt.

"Vicar say, God be all right if she passed out them charms, and he offered to help her." Charity hesitated as she lit the pipe, drawing a few puffs.

"You know, I don't want you thinkin' for a minute that the Vicar had any choice in what he was about to do. You know well as I, we all just gettin' dragged around by that girl. We sooner to later figurin' out, it ain't about what we thinkin' we done, we just doin' what Pearl want all along. That all I'm gonna say about Pearl's charms. It's up to Pearl to tell the rest. Don't be thinkin' the Vicar gonna say anything 'cause he got a promise to Pearl."

Charity stopped and puffed on her pipe as three men with lanterns drew near. Charity recognized them as three of the camp slaves and smiled at them.

"You boys goin' down to the river to catch your breakfast?"

"Yes, Miss Charity, boss man give us his rifle in case we see a 'coon or 'possum," one of the men responded.

Charity chuckled. "Don't you forget them half shell 'possum. They good eatin'; you cook 'em right."

"Why, Miss Charity, you know I don't like no half-shell 'possum. When you gonna make us a pot o' that stew we been smellin' all day?" the man asked.

"Soon enough. That pot you smell today was for Miss Pearl. She have a guest and a good trusted friend, Mr. Brandon, visitin' from Apalach."

The three men stopped by the fire. Charity introduced one of them as John Davis, a crew leader.

"Nice to meet you, Mr. Brandon. I heard Miss Pearl go on and on about you, and that make you good with me."

"You know," he let out a short laugh before he continued. "If everybody in the world was to think like our Miss Pearl, everybody would get along, and they wouldn't be no war. The danger would be people talkin' themselves to death; they be droppin' all over the place." Knowing Pearl, we all shared a good laugh.

The three men wandered on toward the river. John yelled back to Charity. "I sure be glad when it warm up and them 'cooters and 'gators come back out, so we can get some proper food."

Charity puffed on her pipe. "Back to Pearl; we need to watch out after our girl 'cause she still got lots to do," she told me. "We got to help her when we can 'cause Pearl has an old soul. She follows a path and lives a life Jesus lay down all them years ago."

"I agree with you, Miss Charity," I told her.

"It a path few can follow, but she born with the understandin' of a child, and she refuse to change even though the world think she should. It 'cause she hold on to that understandin' that she still walkin' the path."

"I'm starting to see that Miss Charity," I told her.

"I tell you all this 'cause old Charity feel herself fadin' and know it ain't long 'fore I be called home, leavin' this world behind. Miss Pearl gonna need people to care for her, and that gonna be you and Miss Caroline."

"We'll do our best," I said.

"I see a danger lurkin' in the shadows. Pearl's papa, he heard about some charm she been passin' out, and he been askin' her to bring him one. She keep tellin' him he don't need one 'cause he got her, and 'cause o' that, he be a rich man. I just don't know how long she can hold him off."

"I wish he hadn't taken her away from Apalachicola," I told her. "We miss her something dreadful."

"He been runnin' around with them men callin' theyselves the Rebel Guard. They got nothin' to do with the soldiers fightin'. They just a buncha ruffians, goin' around robbin' and killin' folks, sayin' they representin' the government. But all they doin' is fillin' they pockets. Watch out for these men; you can tell 'em by a small owl feather they carry on they hats. They done robbed and killed everywhere else, and I'm afeared you gonna' be seein' a lot more a them in Apalach."

We sat for a while contemplating, but Miss Charity wasn't through.

"You probably wonderin' why an old nigger woman be up here in the woods makin' soap for the very people be keepin' her a slave all her life. Fact is, my youngest boy Milton, he up in Tennessee right now. Our master, Mr. Orman, my boy's daddy, sent him up with his white son, Mr. William Orman, to help look after and take care o' him. Last I heard about Milton was in a letter, where Mr. William say Milton doin' good and rollin' in the fat. I pray ever day Milton still rollin' in that fat."

"I'll pray he is still well off too," I said, wondering how the war was going on in far-away places.

"That why I smoke this pipe," Miss Charity told me. "It belong to Mr. William Orman. It was his pipe 'til the lady's nose got half broke off, and he don't want it no more. My boy Milton tell Mr. William how his mama like smokin' a pipe, so he get that pipe and give it to me as a gift. I smoke it 'cause it remind me of my son Milton."

She hesitated a moment, puffing the pipe, thinking of her son, and in a strong voice told me, "You gotta quit waitin', and do what's proper by Miss Caroline. You get that girl to the church, and make it right by her. I'll stay here for the time bein' and keep an eye on our Pearl, and I will promise you, with God as my witness, I will return her to Apalach. The rest gonna be up to you."

I sat for a moment, dumbfounded.

"I hate to be tellin' you this, but your wagon is loaded, and your mules is hitched. You need ta be headin' for the Narrows. I know you ain't had no sleep, but them mules know the way, and you can sleep a little as you ride."

"You're right about that," I told her.

"Pearl and me, we gonna be travelin' some today, so she won't be here when you pass back by, but don't you be worryin', 'cause it won't be long 'fore she back in Apalach."

"I'll hold you to that," I said.

"Fore you go, have a sip o' this." She picked up a jug, pulled the cork, and poured a small glass which she handed to me.

"This keep you warm this mornin' in your travels. I brew this myself, and it make me kinda famous."

I took a sip of the amber liquid. It turned out to be the best scuppernong wine I had ever tasted. I finished the glass with a toast to Miss Charity. Good scuppernong wine was highly prized for its smooth flavor. When I stood to leave, an overwhelming feeling of warmth moved through my entire body.

***

The early morning was crisp, the moon so bright that the mules navigated the trail without a lantern. I turned occasionally to watch as the camp fires faded into darkness. It was a good trail, mostly straight from the camp to the Narrows.

I don't remember much of the journey. I nodded off several times, stirred from time to time by a few rough patches in the road. Fact is, I slept most of the entire way. If it hadn't been for the mules stopping at the edge of the river, I may have drowned.

I hate to admit it, but the first thing I saw when I opened my eyes at the Narrows was Hatch's face grinning at me. He watched me arrive sound asleep.

"It's a good thing I ain't a rattlesnake, or I'd a bit ya," he told me. "You were snoring like a hound dog."

# Chapter IX

## The Proposal

I jumped down from the wagon, gave Hatch a hug, and patted him on the shoulders. I called him an old so and so and told him when I got to the camp and found out what I was sent for, I had come up with a few choice words for my old friend Captain Hatch. But things changed a lot after I got to the soap works.

"I want to thank you for what you did, brother. You don't know how much that meant to me."

"Oh, don't give it a thought Michael," Hatch shrugged it off. "Last time I was at your house, you whined so much about Pearl this and Pearl that, I felt it my duty to do something about it. I figured if I told you, you'd come up anyway, so I thought you might just as well make yourself useful and haul a little freight for your good friend Hatch."

I shook my head at him. "Hatch you are incorrigible," I fired back.

"I know, and you are welcome," Hatch's tone was sincere. There was no need to go on. I didn't stand a chance with Hatch on the receiving end of a conversation.

We unloaded the wagon's contents onto a small, steam-powered skiff. We then loaded four wooden crates into the back of the wagon. I was instructed not to open them until back home with Caroline.

Hatch shoved off. As he moved away from shore, he yelled, "I'll be back in town April eighteenth for the wedding."

"Whose wedding?"

"Yours, of course. I'll bring my best suit. I'm your best man, and don't forget the ring. Best man will need that to do a good job."

"What makes you so sure I'm getting married on April eighteenth?"

"'Cause it's the day I'll be back in town. I can't keep that gal of yours waiting on me forever."

He waved as his boat puffed up the river. My heart sank as he rounded the first bend, and I lost sight of him. I could not bear the thought of a future without my flap-jawed friend.

I turned the wagon toward home. If I traveled steady and stopped only to rest the mules, I could be at Caroline's for supper by eight o'clock. I looked forward to the look on her face when I walked in, then again when I told her my news. The weather was clear and bright. I would not have doubted that this day was an answer to one of Pearl's prayers. I was also looking forward to my bed; sleeping in a moving wagon was a younger man's game.

I arrived at Caroline's at ten after eight. Caroline threw her arms around me.

She must have forgiven me for my silence earlier. In her embrace, I could feel my tension drifting away.

She led me to a table and signaled for the food to be served.

"You must be starved."

"I was, but after seeing you, not so much anymore."

"You have such a honey tongue. Let's get you fed; we have lots to catch up on."

I was starving but bursting with news, so I ate quickly. She tried to slow me down, saying she worried about my digestion. I finished and washed down the meal with a long drink.

"I saw Pearl," I told her.

Caroline brought her hand up to cover her mouth. Her eyes began to tear. Suddenly, she reached out and smacked me on the shoulder.

"What did you do that for?" I asked.

"You were sitting there with news like that, and you didn't tell me." She put her hand back over her mouth and wriggled in her chair as if ready to burst.

"Get your drink, come outside, and tell me everything. Is she all right?"

"Pearl is good. She's with Miss Charity up in the pine forest, making soap at the old turpentine camp. Pearl's the only real reason that flap-jawed friend of mine sent me up there in the first place."

Caroline smiled. "God bless him and his little flap-jawed ways." Caroline pressed me for every little detail of my journey.

"I wish I had been there and seen Pearl."

I told her everything I could remember but left out the part about a wedding.

"What is the news of this town?" I was able to ask when she was content.

"I think I was nearly attacked," she said, looking me straight in the eye.

"You waited to tell me that?" I reached over and poked her on the arm.

"You're the one who had the great adventure; besides Stillman was there, and nothing happened."

"Tell me about it." I was now as eager as she had been before the news about Pearl.

"You know, as well as I, that business at the Florida House has been slow, at best."

It certainly had been slow. Occasionally, a steamer traveling the coastline, after inspection by the blockade, would arrive in town, and the four rooms of the Florida Boarding House would once again come to life. The spacious rooms contained three beds each, but additional cots accommodated more guests during events.

"On the afternoon of the day you left, a man arrived at the Florida House. No one other than local oystermen had arrived in port, so the stranger must have walked into town. His dress and a long whip on his belt indicated that he was a cracker cowboy from the central prairies of the state. In Apalach, he was out of place, and it made no sense," said Caroline.

She described his manner as twitchy and his stature as short and stocky. He requested a room and meals and said he would depart after breakfast next morning, signing the book simply, Aldridge. He stowed his gear and wandered around the town, looking in shops and through the windows of buildings closed since the beginning of the war.

"Very few guests arrived for the evening meal, just some locals and this strange visitor. He seemed to enjoy the meal and appeared to understand about the shortages. He offered no complaint with substitutions offered during the meal. He left after eating and disappeared into town."

Caroline was staying at the house on Cedar Street that I had brought from St. Joseph. At this point, curious, but not overly concerned about the stranger, she hurried home in the dusk. As she unlocked the door, she heard the squeak of a loose step. She turned and was startled by the sight of her lodger standing on the lower step.

***

"What are you doing here? This is my home."

"No need for concern Miss; I'm here under orders from my commander to look the town over for supplies for our troops," Aldridge responded. "I'll be inspecting all the homes in the area for food and weapons that might help the war effort. I'll need to take a look inside now."

"The hell you will! Get off my property," shouted Caroline, outraged.

Aldridge advanced a step. Looking at Caroline, he said, "Afraid that won't be possible."

Caroline was trembling as she told me about this. Her hand clutching mine was like a vise.

As Aldridge reached the third step, Stillman, with a load of firewood in one arm and his ax in hand, called out in a loud voice, "Miss Caroline, I chopped this wood for your fire. You want I should put it in the house?"

Aldridge, startled, pulled a bowie knife as he turned on Stillman. Six feet is all that separated the two men.

Stillman lowered his arm, dropping the wood. Gripping the ax in both hands, he glared at Aldridge. In a calm voice, Stillman told him,

"Miss Caroline has done asked you to leave her property. It be up to you 'cause if it be up to me, I ain't a gonna ask."

Aldridge looked at the ax in Stillman's hands and decided his knife was not big enough. He backed away into the darkness.

Caroline made coffee, and she and Stillman sat on the porch and talked until two o'clock.

"I'll stand watch," Stillman told her. "You go on in and get some rest."

Caroline went inside, but the door opened as she handed Stillman the Colt Paterson I left behind. "I just hate these things. Would you mind keeping it out here with you? Michael said it's loaded, so be careful."

"I will. Good night Miss," said Stillman.

***

The rest of the night was quiet, Caroline told me. Aldridge must have been acting alone, casing the town.

The next morning, Stillman and I spoke at length about the incident. He confirmed my fears. Aldridge had worn a small owl feather in the brim of his hat. He was on reconnaissance for the Rebel Guard.

I could not thank Stillman enough for his bravery, but he was probably now marked for death by the guard. A black man raising an ax against a white man would find no forgiveness. I offered to hide him out at the Customs House for a few days in case this had been an isolated incident. He refused. I suggested that, for his own sake, he ask for asylum with the blockade forces, offering to go with him to help explain the circumstances. Again, he refused. I then insisted he move in with me at my Cedar Street house. We could establish safety in numbers by setting up a proper watch.

I feared for Jacob's mother Jenny. Alone, she was an easy target. In similar danger were Ava and Lottie, the young girls who staffed the Florida House. I told Caroline we would pay a visit to Jenny and convince her to move into the old home place on Laurel. With Ava and Lottie, they could find safety under our watch. When we had boarders at the Florida House, one of the two girls could stay in their room above the restaurant. With boarders, they should be safe enough.

Caroline refused to yield to the threat posed by Aldridge or the Rebel Guard he represented. She insisted on keeping her schedules.

"If I change my ways, evil will have already triumphed," she pointed out.

While Caroline worked, Stillman kept watch over the houses. I spent the day warning townspeople of the impending threat. Friends and neighbors agreed to watch out for one another.

I was standing at the door of the Florida House when Caroline walked out. I think she was relieved to see me there, ready to walk her home. She pointed over to her restaurant next door to the Florida House. The restaurant faced Centre Street with its back porch facing the Florida House. She had connected a rope from an upstairs window, where Lottie and Ava stayed, to the dinner bell on the back porch roof. The girls could ring the bell from up or down stairs in the event of trouble.

The next week, I installed a bell on the porch roof of the old home place on Laurel so that an alert could be sounded there.

I decided to move our larder to the Customs House for safekeeping. Stillman and I would load the stores in the wagon early in the morning before townspeople stirred. Then we would pull the wagon by hand to the Florida House and unload. We would return later that night to transfer the cases by hand to the Customs House. The commercial section of Water Street was vacant at night. Many buildings had been boarded up since the war began.

"We should be able to move the goods in two trips," I told Stillman. He was at the door, ready to load before daylight.

"What you want to do with them four crates in the wagon?" He asked.

I had forgotten about the crates Hatch sent back. "Leave them, and we'll unload them with the rest of the cargo."

"What crates?" Caroline had overheard.

"The ones Hatch sent."

"Hatch? Be sure and put the new crates in the kitchen at the restaurant. I want to see what's in them," she said.

"Curiosity killed the cat," I muttered to Stillman.

Everything went as planned, and we pulled the empty wagon in beside my house just as the sun rose over the horizon.

"You want me to stay here and keep an eye on things?" Stillman asked.

Even though I had earlier made light of Caroline's curiosity, I knew Stillman's was just as bad.

"Why don't you come on with me to the restaurant, have some breakfast, and help pry open those crates. Then come back here and keep watch."

"You know best. I'd be happy to help you with the crates," Stillman smiled.

Caroline came down the steps and took me by the arm.

"By the way, why don't you explain about this cat?" Stillman overheard, grinning as he looked back. I never took Caroline's hearing for granted again.

Lottie added a plate for Stillman at a table in the kitchen. I had not given eating arrangements much thought. I didn't want to hurt Stillman's feelings, and I didn't want to face the fact that his presence would not be tolerated out front.

After breakfast, we approached the crates stacked in the corner. I had to laugh out loud. Sometime during the meal, I had lost track of Caroline. Perched on top of the crates was a small pry bar and a hammer. Caroline, hearing me laugh, hugged me.

"Open those crates before I burst," she whispered.

The first crate was heavy with items we had not seen in a long while. Bags of flour, sugar, bottles of vanilla extract, pepper, spices we had never seen before, Lea & Perrins® Worcestershire Sauce, bags of dried beans and peas, jars of Underwood pickled vegetables, and pickled mackerel were some of the variety we pulled from the crate.

The second crate was better than the first. We stood in awe when the packing, consisting of more bags of dried beans and flour, revealed four large, cured hams, slabs of smoked bacon, and kegs of salted fatback.

Stillman and I stood with eyes big as saucers when out of the packing of the third crate came bottles of red and white wine, fine whiskey, brandy, port, sherry, boxes of cigars, tobacco, and bag after bag of coffee and tea. The crate even contained a copper humidor, several new pipes, a couple of tins of black powder, and a new Colt Navy revolver. Caroline was noticeably not as pleased with the contents of this crate as were Stillman and I.

The fourth crate was the smallest. Prying the lid, we found an envelope on which was the name Michael. Caroline offered it to me. I was busy examining the cigars with Stillman and acknowledged that she should go ahead and read it.

"Michael, thank you for watching over my family and Apalach while I am away," Caroline read aloud. "My hope is that these crates contain most of the items you requested. I look forward to your wedding. See you on 18 April 1863, your friend, your brother, Hatch."

I felt a catch in my throat. What was he up to? I dropped what I was holding, staring at the fourth crate as Caroline removed the packing. Buttons, laces, thread, sewing needles, and bolts of fabric appeared. Peering over her shoulder, I watched as she sorted through, stroking the fabrics with her hand.

Caroline looked at me with tears welling from her eyes. Before I could explain, she hugged and kissed me in front of everyone, patting my cheeks and proclaiming me a wonderful man. She was crying. Ava and Lottie were crying. Even Stillman, my only source of support, was rubbing his eyes, and now to all present, I was officially getting married on 18 April 1863.

*I would have eventually gotten around to setting a date,* I thought.

Looking back, thanks to Hatch's presence of mind, I now stood immortalized in the eyes of not only the women present, but also, within one day, I would be immortalized in the eyes of every woman in town. Hatch knew I was clumsy when it came to matters of the heart. This is an accurate record of this event. I never mustered the backbone to tell her the truth, and to his credit, Hatch never said a word.

The crates contained all the makings for a wedding celebration, and within the scattered packing were memories of happier times before the war when the town searched for any reason to hold a celebration. A good wedding could be just what the town needed to bring its people together. If even for a fleeting moment, we could once again feel normal.

# Chapter X

## Emancipation

Off in the distance, two steamboats sounded whistles as they headed into port. Caroline and the girls began to busy themselves, getting ready for visitors. Stillman and I returned the items to their crates; keeping out a few necessities, we headed back home.

I sat on the porch while Stillman retrieved a couple of glasses from the house. It was a long while since I had sipped a fine bourbon or smoked a good cigar. Although we both knew it to be inappropriate, nonetheless, here we were, at ten o'clock in the morning, sipping fine bourbon whiskey and smoking a good cigar.

Stillman was admiring the 1851 Navy Colt.

"Mr. Brandon, a finer piece of weaponry I have never seen," he stated.

I loaded the Colt, holstered it, and handed it to Stillman. "Man like you, lacking in good sense, taking the chances you do, needs a good weapon he can call his own. Be sure to take that extra powder and shot. Get yourself familiar with that new pistol of yours. You best take your choice of the pipes and a pouch of tobacco to help keep you awake at night."

Stillman gazed down at the Colt in his hands. "Mr. Brandon, a finer gift I have never received."

I could no longer view Stillman as anything other than a friend. I advised him to conceal the pistol in order to avoid attracting unwanted attention.

"Stillman, you know over the years, there's been lots of talk about slavery. Mr. Lincoln, as early as September last year, sent out a proclamation that stipulated if the South did not cease their rebellion by January 1, 1863, his Emancipation Proclamation would pass into law, freeing all slaves held in rebellious states.

"I don't have word yet that this happened. I never owned a slave in my life, so I suppose I never felt it had much to do with me. I'm beginning to think feeling that way was wrong. I just want you to know, no matter the outcome of this war, I will make it a point to see you live somewhere as a free man."

"Mr. Brandon, those words you speakin', they now the finest gift I ever received, including this here Navy Colt."

I extended my hand to shake his. "I know, for your own safety, it's best around people that you call me Mr. Brandon, but when it's just us, my name is Michael."

"I have to say, Michael, you give me hope for a future." Stillman told me. "How about we have another sip of that fine bourbon whiskey 'fore we get back to business."

Just after midnight, one crate at a time, Stillman and I carried our food stores from the Florida House down to the Customs House. Unobserved, we secured the crates in the new larder, my former office. When we finished at three-thirty a.m., we walked back down toward High Street for a final check of the Florida and Jenny boarding houses and found all was quiet. We returned home to my Cedar Street house and took turns on watch.

\*\*\*

It was a good day for Caroline and the girls at the Florida House. Business was brisk. Lottie and Ava spent the night in the room above the restaurant to take better care of our guests. With the rooms of the boarding house occupied, they would be safe enough. That evening,

Stillman kept an eye on my houses while Caroline and I walked over to the Foley home on Market and Broad Streets to have a talk with Jenny.

Jenny felt uneasy since she heard of Caroline's encounter with Aldridge, and it wasn't hard to convince her to move. We agreed she should pack her things this very night, and we would move her over the next morning.

I suggested to Caroline and Jenny that in these hard times, it would be advantageous for us to consolidate the Florida House and Jenny's boarding house and run them as one.

"With the help of Lottie and Ava, we could do a more efficient job of running both houses," I suggested.

Caroline and Jenny agreed and quickly moved on to the more pressing business of matrimony.

In a conversation I once dominated, I now felt myself an albatross in the room. I walked out onto the porch unnoticed while inside they continued to address wedding plans. How humble was my mind? How could I have been under the false impression that getting married was simple?

Early the next morning, with Stillman pushing and me steering and pulling, we moved the wagon four blocks to Jenny Foley's home on the corner of Market and Broad.

This neighborhood bordered the Florida Promenade near the Live Oak Grove and was one of the first areas most folks abandoned when the war started because of its proximity to the bay.

Miss Jenny greeted us and insisted on helping to load her belongings. Once the load was secured, we pulled the wagon back toward my house on Laurel.

Caroline met us as we approached the house and took Jenny by the hand, welcomed her, and invited her for tea while Stillman and I unloaded the wagon.

Over the next few days, everyone settled in nicely to the new arrangements.

\*\*\*

The Union blockade returned to town January 16, 1863. The officer commanding the detachment announced the Emancipation Proclamation passed and had been signed into law January 1, 1863.

The officer read the document to all gathered and ordered his men to post copies on the buildings along the wharf. In the eyes of the North, this document carried the power to free all slaves held in Confederate states. He announced that emancipated slaves of our area would be sent south by steamer to the Keys where they could find work in agriculture. The officer, an excellent orator, committed the document to memory and presented a stage-worthy performance. If Lincoln authored the document, it was a testimony to his wherewithal and insight. After the proceedings, I pulled a copy from a wall in feigned dismay, a ruse for some who might be watching. But in fact, I was eager to examine the document more closely. I walked briskly back home, looking forward to Stillman's rejoinder.

Stillman was busying himself fixing the porch roof on the Cedar Street house when he spotted me coming two blocks away. I watched him climb back through the upstairs window. By the time I reached the yard, he was there to greet me.

"Mr. Michael, what in the world is goin' on? People been walkin' by, hurryin' to get downtown. I'm setting up on that roof just bustin' to find out why."

Stillman had to sense my excitement when I pointed. "Inside," I said.

I sat at the kitchen table. Stillman walked over to the stove and poured us some coffee. As he put the cups on the table, I held up the piece of paper.

"Yanks were in town making an announcement this morning. I'd like to read you a proclamation. It's from Mr. Lincoln."

# The Emancipation Proclamation January 1, 1863

*By the President of the United States of
America:
A Proclamation.*

*Whereas, on the twenty-second day of
September, in the year of our Lord one thousand
eight hundred and sixty-two, a proclamation
was issued by the President of the United
States, containing, among other things, the
following, to wit:*

*That on the first day of January, in the year
of our Lord one thousand eight hundred and
sixty-three, all persons held as slaves within
any State or designated part of a State, the
people whereof shall then be in rebellion against
the United States, shall be then, thenceforward,
and forever free; and the Executive Government
of the United States, including the military and
naval authority thereof, will recognize and
maintain the freedom of such persons, and will
do no act or acts to repress such persons, or any
of them, in any efforts they may make for their
actual freedom.*

*That the Executive will, on the first day of
January aforesaid, by proclamation, designate
the States and parts of States, if any, in which
the people thereof, respectively, shall then be in
rebellion against the United States; and the fact
that any State, or the people thereof, shall on*

*that day be, in good faith, represented in the Congress of the United States by members chosen thereto at elections wherein a majority of the qualified voters of such State shall have participated, shall, in the absence of strong countervailing testimony, be deemed conclusive evidence that such State, and the people thereof, are not then in rebellion against the United States."*

*Now, therefore I, Abraham Lincoln, President of the United States, by virtue of the power in me vested as Commander-in-Chief, of the Army and Navy of the United States in time of actual armed rebellion against the authority and government of the United States, and as a fit and necessary war measure for suppressing said rebellion, do, on this first day of January, in the year of our Lord one thousand eight hundred and sixty-three, and in accordance with my purpose so to do publicly proclaimed for the full period of one hundred days, from the day first above mentioned, order and designate as the States and parts of States wherein the people thereof respectively, are this day in rebellion against the United States, the following, to wit:*

*Arkansas, Texas, Louisiana, (except the Parishes of St. Bernard,. Plaquemines, Jefferson, St. John, St. Charles, St. James Ascension, Assumption, Terrebonne, Lafourche, St. Mary, St. Martin, and Orleans, including the City of New Orleans), Mississippi, Alabama, Florida, Georgia, South Carolina, North Carolina, and Virginia, (except the forty-eight counties designated as West Virginia, and also the counties of Berkley, Accomac, Northampton, Elizabeth City, York, Princess Ann, and Norfolk, including the cities of Norfolk and Portsmouth), and which excepted parts, are for the present, left precisely as if this proclamation were not issued.*

*And by virtue of the power, and for the purpose aforesaid, I do order and declare that all persons held as slaves within said designated States, and parts of States, are, and henceforward shall be free; and that the Executive government of the United States, including the military and naval authorities thereof, will recognize and maintain the freedom of said persons.*

*And I hereby enjoin upon the people so declared to be free to abstain from all violence, unless in necessary self-defense; and I recommend to them that, in all cases when allowed, they labor faithfully for reasonable wages.*

*And I further declare and make known, that such persons of suitable condition, will be received into the armed service of the United States to garrison forts, positions, stations, and other places, and to man vessels of all sorts in said service.*

*And upon this act, sincerely believed to be an act of justice, warranted by the Constitution, upon military necessity, I invoke the considerate judgment of mankind, and the gracious favor of Almighty God.*

*In witness whereof, I have hereunto set my hand and caused the seal of the United States to be affixed.*

*Done at the City of Washington, this first day of January, in the year of our Lord one thousand eight hundred and sixty three, and of the Independence of the United States of America the eighty-seventh.*

*By the President: ABRAHAM LINCOLN*
*WILLIAM H. SEWARD, Secretary of State.*

Stillman listened intently to every word of the proclamation, and then raised his hands. "Lord have mercy. Just imagine, this day, a people of bondage get their first hope of freedom."

He thought for a moment. "That is if Mr. Lincoln win. Otherwise, with or without North and South, all around the world the battle for freedom will go on until every man walk free. It in the nature of man to be free, and no man, whether he be master or slave, will know true freedom until it be declared for all men."

I raised my hands in frustration, and in a blind stare tried to give voice to all my sordid thoughts.

"I've been troubled trying to consider all the whys and wherefores that could justify this war," I said.

"Early on, I felt some reasons worth fighting for. I always believed the South under the Constitution had the right to secede. Now, in hindsight, knowing hundreds of thousands are dying, there was no cause great enough to justify this war. Of one thing I am now certain, sitting here today, with God as my witness, I can no longer abide slavery. If that makes me a Yankee, so be it. You know I was solemn when I told you, no matter what, I will see that you live as a free man," I told Stillman.

"Michael, who'da thought in these times, you and me bein' friends? You know with what high regard I hold Miss Caroline. Fact is, I care about all your friends; because to them my color don't seem to make no difference," Stillman said.

"Ya'all are like my own family. Now, I don't want you frettin' none, but I got thoughts been troubling my mind, and some half-truths been weighing heavy on my conscience. I need to be confessing these things to you and Miss Caroline, but this ain't the time now. I need to think on it a while longer and maybe grow me a little more backbone. But it's important you know, in case something bad happens to me." I could see the despair in his eyes as he pondered thoughts I could only imagine.

"If you feel the need, you tell me anything, but you owe me nothing," I said, trying to ease his fears.

\*\*\*

Distance protected Apalachicola from the carnage of battle. Offshore, we were at the mercy of an impenetrable Union blockade. A small Confederate force still controlled the river to the north, with reconnoiters to Apalachicola recording the movements of the Union Navy. Those citizens remaining in Apalachicola walked a fine line, falling under the scrutiny of the Union blockade offshore and the Confederacy up the river, but the real perceived threat came from neither. The threat that shadowed the town still came from the group of ruffians calling themselves the Rebel Guard. Reports of piracy and death followed in the wake of their movements across the Florida Panhandle.

Perhaps the Union presence offshore was the deterrent that up to now had kept them at bay, but this presence was undergoing a change that could inflame the Rebel Guard and draw them down river to Apalachicola. Over the last few months, most of the white blockade regiments found themselves reassigned north and replaced with United States Colored Troops—U.S.C.T. regiments.

Adding insult to injury, plantation masters now found themselves held hostage by the very slaves who once worked their lands. Free Northern blacks and runaway slaves would soon make up a large percentage of blockade regiments. In the eyes of a Union seaman, blockading Florida ports was one of the more boring duties of the war.

Still, Union sailors sought these positions because bounty taken from captured blockade vessels went to auction. Portions of profits were divvied up among the crew according to rank, making it a boring but profitable duty.

\*\*\*

Much to my chagrin, in order to avoid the appearance of impropriety, Caroline moved into the Laurel Street house with Jenny, Ava, and Lottie. Preparations were well under way for the wedding. Lights burned late into the night as the women sewed in anticipation of the date.

During the changing of the guard, Stillman and I stayed alert by deliberating events and making plans over a sip of scotch and a bowl of tobacco. My friend altered my perception of the world. The supposedly illiterate, former slave never ceased to amaze me with his perceptions. Some nights we sat on the porch and talked until morning, catching some sleep after the town began to stir.

Normal was not a word that applied to life under siege. Understanding came to me when I considered Pearl, a little girl who accepted and thrived in an intolerable life because she knew no difference. The town was learning to exist with our captors, accepting these hard times as the new normal.

The magnitude of my proposal to Caroline began affecting my digestion on April 10, 1863. It didn't help that the upcoming wedding had become a major event, and all of the town's remaining citizens were reminding me of a date fast approaching. I was awkward with large groups, preferring small gatherings, and this was shaping up to be anything but a small event.

# Chapter XI

## Rebel Guard & The Revelation

Our darkest hours began in the early morning of Monday, April 13, 1863. Stillman woke me.

"Michael, you need to grab onto those Patersons and follow me." We made our way down the darkened stairs and out onto the porch. "It be best if we stay in the shadows and watch from here," he whispered.

What was left of a quarter moon dimly illuminated the outline of neighboring houses. Stillman pointed across the street, "Watch over there on the corner of that house off of Cedar Street."

We sat in darkness for what seemed like eternity but in reality was a few minutes. Suddenly, from beside the empty house, a match strike revealed a presence. As the match rose to light a pipe, the dim glow lit up a face. I did not recognize the man, but Stillman now gripped my arm and pointed.

"That be Aldridge," he said.

Aldridge held the match over, lighting the cigar of a second man. This man I knew. My blood curdled in my veins at the sight of Dray. Before Aldridge shook out the match light, it burned just long enough to cast shadows on the neighboring house, marking the presence of two other men.

From inside my house, I heard the faint chime of the mantle clock sounding half past. The men muttered, and at times, you could almost make out a word or two.

"Michael, if you ever trusted me, then trust me now. If those men come this way, you need to stand behind that porch post and fire that big old Paterson twice up in the air."

I did not understand his reasoning, but he seemed to be anticipating the Rebel Guards' next move. I had never been in a situation like this before. Stillman seemed confident, so I responded, "Say when."

The muttering continued, and then as though they were listening to the same chime, the clock struck three, and four men came out of the shadows and headed directly toward us.

"They don't know we're here. Stay in the shadow of the post and fire when I tell you," Stillman alerted me.

I rose to my feet and in the shadows positioned myself behind the post.

As the men entered the street, Stillman whispered: "Fire."

The Paterson, loud in the daytime, seemed like a cannon in the quiet night. The Guard crouched in the street, contemplating their next move. In houses blocks away, lights were appearing. You could hear doors opening in the darkness. Stillman's plan became obvious. The odds were no longer in the Rebel Guards' favor. They were out-gunned and lost their element of surprise. We watched as they retreated down the street.

The women stood on the porch of the Laurel Street house, I think hoping for the best but expecting the worst. Stillman and I walked to neighbors' houses nearby to let them know what happened. We advised everyone to remain vigilant and to fire a shot if they suspected trouble.

"Stillman, if I had a medal, I'd pin it on you right now. How'd you know that would work?

"Mr. Brandon, don't be pinning no medal on me yet 'cause it might be over tonight, but it has just begun."

We all stayed close in to the house until the sun lit the horizon. Stillman kept watch while I walked the women to work. I checked Water Street down to the Bowery but saw no sign of Dray or Aldridge and kept an eye peeled for owl feathers.

At home, Stillman cooked a breakfast with eggs and bacon and prepared a pot of collards in fatback.

"I know it's early in the day for greens, but being up all night has given me a powerful cravin'. I hope you don't mind," he said, as I walked in the door.

"After last night, if you told me you had a craving for elephant steak, I'd go out and see if I could find one."

We moved onto the porch to eat so we could keep a better eye on the property. Neighbors walking by joined us for a cup of coffee, wanting to talk about the events of the early morning. They all agreed the gunshots were a good warning. We laughed about the Rebel Guard running down the street, but inside, we shuddered at the thought of what might have been.

"I think when Miss Caroline get home, we need to have us that talk," Stillman told me, with a troubled look.

"We can have that talk this evening, but right now, you need to go in that house and get some sleep. I'll keep watch for a few hours."

Stillman went inside for a well-desired rest. I put the unfired Colt on the table and began to load the empty chambers of the gun I had fired. I thought about what might have happened had it not been for Stillman's quick thinking.

I held the gun in my hands and imagined the consequences of a bullet ripping through the body of another human being. To take the sacred right of life and death, reserved only for the wisdom of God, and place that decision in the hand of a man with a gun, troubled me greatly.

I would like to think that in the defense of my loved ones, I could pull the trigger, but I prayed I would never have to find out.

Stillman woke at eleven o'clock in the morning, and much to his objection, I insisted we walk downtown and look around, and then go to the restaurant for dinner. In the back of my mind, I thought the Rebel Guard might pay a visit while we were away. I had imagined them raiding and burning my house then going away and leaving us in peace. I would consider that a small price to pay.

The Rebel Guard was conspicuous by their absence, but I felt them in the shadow of every abandoned cotton warehouse.

Caroline greeted us at the restaurant.

"Made more than we could eat, hate for them to go to waste." Stillman handed her the pot of greens he had prepared.

Caroline took the pot. "I have a couple of travelers who will make short work of these."

We sat out back of the restaurant in the shade of a water oak. Caroline put us to work shucking a few dozen oysters for her customers, and we also shucked a couple of dozen for ourselves, sliding them down with a little New York hot sauce provided courtesy of Hatch.

"I wonder how Hatch came upon bottles of J. McCollick Bird Pepper Sauce and Lea & Perrins® Worcestershire Sauce. Haven't seen things like these since the war began," I said.

We laughed, thinking of Hatch as a Yankee trader. We knew he had pulled a lot of strings to get us the crates of supplies.

"I'll bet somewhere in New York City, they is some rich Yank enjoyin' a Shaddock with his breakfast," said Stillman.

"Imagine that, some rich Yank, savoring a juicy grapefruit," I said.

Holding up oysters, we toasted. "To Hatch Wefing, the old Yankee trader."

Caroline heard us laughing and smiled to herself as she approached with a couple of bowls of her best oyster stew, fresh baked bread, and glasses of sweet tea. Considering wartime prices and tea going at thirty dollars a pound, Stillman and I continued loafing for a couple more hours, feeling like kings with nothing better to do than pass the time of day.

I suggested we might want to consider moving into the Florida House until we were sure the Rebel Guard was no longer a threat. Stillman pointed out the boarding houses were in an area that at night was more isolated and would make us an easy target. I told him what I knew of Dray and of the incident over twenty years ago when I was so wrought up after digging the bodies of my parents out of a burial pit. I wondered if this might have some bearing on why we were apparently being targeted.

"I've seen chain of command before, and when I saw those men walking across the street, I could tell Dray is the leader, and Aldridge is one of his lieutenants. I guarantee you; Aldridge ain't gonna forget he got bested by us," said Stillman.

We returned home before sunset, first checking the Laurel house so Lottie, Ava, and Jenny could settle in for the night. Caroline, Stillman, and I went next door to my house on Cedar Street and sat talking on the front porch so we could keep an eye on both houses.

Stillman sat with an elbow on his knee, rubbing his forehead with his hand, then looked up. He hesitated, holding his hand below his mouth, stroking his whiskers. A few moments passed. Then he spoke.

"I am, and will forever, be your friend. If I have known better people than you and your friends, I cannot remember. You have shattered everything I believed about people of the South. I would never do or say anything to intentionally put you in harm's way, but I now fear that unintentionally, I did just that."

Caroline and I glanced at each other in shock at the changes we now witnessed. Stillman's vocabulary, his diction, and even his very presence was altered. I knew the confused look on Caroline's face was a mirror image of my own.

"The Fugitive Slave Act of September 18, 1850 is where it all started to change for me. I was not able to tell you until now, but I have a wife and two young daughters. Before the war, I was a teacher."

Caroline could tell this came hard for Stillman. She offered him a smile of reassurance and patted his hand before he continued.

"I'll get to them later," he said. "My name is Stillman Smith. I was born a free black in Middlebury, Vermont. My father, whom I love dearly, was a jack-of-all-trades who taught me all I needed to make my way in this world. My mama convinced him there was more to this world than just learning a good trade. My mother and father worked their fingers to the bone to send me to the best schools. They hired tutors to help me with my lessons and sent me off to Middlebury College in Vermont. "Imagine that." He sat contemplating for a moment.

"Alexander Lucius Twilight was my mentor and hero. He was the first black man in the United States to earn a bachelor's degree from an American college. He graduated from Middlebury College in 1823. He died in 1857, but during his time, he was a force to be reckoned with. A

110

fiery minister, principal of a grammar school, and in 1836, he was the first black American elected as a state legislator. He served in the Vermont General Assembly." Stillman shook his head.

"The United States Congress passed The Fugitive Slave Act on September 18, 1850. The act was a part of the Compromise of 1850— compromise worked out between Southern slave-holding interests and Northern Free-Soilers. The Fugitive Slave Act was the most controversial element of the 1850 compromise and heightened Northern fears of a 'slave power conspiracy.' It required that all escaped slaves, upon capture, be returned to their masters. The act required that officials and citizens of Free States had to assist in the implementation of this law. Abolitionists nicknamed it the 'Bloodhound Law' for the dogs they used to track down runaway slaves.

"Alexander Lucius Twilight fought against the Fugitive Slave Act and believed it to be unconstitutional. In order to fight this travesty of justice, in November of 1850, the same year the Fugitive Slave Act passed and became federal law, the Vermont Legislature approved the "Habeas Corpus Law," which required Vermont judicial and law enforcement officials to assist captured fugitive slaves. Habeas Corpus took the bite out of the Fugitive Slave Act. President Millard Fillmore, who had earlier created and signed the Fugitive Slave Act into law, was furious and threatened to use the army to enforce the Fugitive Slave Act in Vermont, but it was all just pomposity, and nothing ever came of it."

"I had heard of that," I said.

Stillman nodded his head.

"Habeas Corpus was a good law. Vermont abolished slavery in the state on July 8, 1777 and did not intend to export any of its black citizens anywhere. Making a law is one thing, enforcing it is another, especially when money is involved. The bounty for blacks was high enough for slavers to justify kidnapping. It didn't matter if you had papers. If they could get you out of state, they bound you, sent you south, and sold you into slavery." Stillman gave a wry smile.

"My wife is beautiful and precious to me. Slavers came to our home and kidnapped her in December of 1856. A beautiful woman like my wife would fetch a high price in a Southern slave market.

"I managed to catch up to those slavers as they were loading her into a boxcar. The police were right behind them. The slavers fired at me and the police. I was hit twice, once in the shoulder. That bullet went straight through. I was hit once in the calf of my leg. It didn't even slow my pace. I kept going, even after the police stopped to take cover. I pulled one of those slavers from the train and beat him within an inch of his life. The police finally followed my lead, and that day, we liberated three free blacks and two runaways from inside that boxcar, including my wife.

"I knew then it would never stop. If it wasn't my wife, soon it would be my daughters. So when the war broke out in 1861 and the Vermont Legislators asked for volunteers, I signed up. I joined the 8th regiment of the Vermont Volunteers Colored Troops and reported to Camp Holbrook in Brattleboro." Stillman let out a long sigh.

"After training, I left for New York in March of 1862 and by May was with the Union occupation force in New Orleans. I saw some action in Louisiana in June and July. Then they transferred me over to Apalachicola as an agent in August. That is when I met you, Michael, down at the Trinity church."

"Stop right here," said Caroline. "I'm making us a pot of coffee." We waited until she returned. Stillman reached out and patted my knee.

"All right, I'm ready to hear more," said Caroline as she handed us our coffee.

"Okay," said Stillman. "I already know one of your questions, and I do not want you to worry about Hatch. He is a good man. I consider him a friend, same as you. I would never say anything that would jeopardize his safety. I am in this war to make the future safe for my family, and the way to do that is to eliminate slavery. Slavery is a shameful blot on our country, and now that Mr. Lincoln has enacted the Emancipation Proclamation, the complexion of the war will change. European countries abolished slavery years ago. If they once contemplated involvement on behalf of the South, now, with the focus on slavery, they will want nothing to do with it."

"I know that even you and Mr. Hatch no longer feel good about the war fought over commerce that relies on the bondage of an entire race.

Pharaoh tried it with the Jews. It was a bad idea then, and it is a bad idea now."

Stillman must have read my mind. He shifted in his chair.

"You have to believe I have not betrayed you. I report to the Union on places like Orman's land at Owl Creek were he still holds twenty-two slaves or the turpentine camp you visited. I report on what I hear from up river about gun emplacements, Confederate blockade locations, troop movement, and blockade-runners. I also report on the threat of the Rebel Guard to the locals. I am sorry if you feel betrayed or used in some way, but I believe the cause I fight for is worth some lost pride."

Stillman placed his Navy revolver in front of me on the table. "I leave my fate at your mercies. I have always been able to judge the measure of a man. I have known men of wisdom, power, greed, but I have seldom come across men of good conscience. These are the men of peace, including you, Michael."

Stunned, I couldn't answer, so I sat still trying to unravel what he had said.

"I wouldn't hold it against you if out of a sense of duty, you felt the need to shoot me down where I sit or hold me and turn me over to the Confederates up river. It doesn't matter what happens to me; the ball is rolling against slavery, and it won't be stopped. Please believe me when I tell you my concern is for the safety of my family here in Apalach, you, Miss Caroline, and the others.

"I could have walked away, rejoined the blockade, and been free and clear, but I would rather you judge me now than have to live with the knowledge I put all of you in danger. The question is where do we go from here?"

I was struggling to utter some response to Stillman's confession, but my mind was blank. Then Caroline, gazing at Stillman, asked the most appropriate question: "How old are your daughters?"

"Claudia is three, and Beth is five."

"You must miss them terribly." Caroline rose and patted Stillman on the shoulder as she passed by. "I think I'll get myself another cup of coffee. I'd imagine my boys would prefer something a little stronger?"

"Right now, a bottle and a couple of glasses would suit me fine,'" I told Caroline, adding, "You can join us if you feel the need."

"I'll just stick to coffee," Caroline smiled, touching my cheek.

I looked at Stillman and shook my head in disbelief. I pushed the Navy revolver back across the table. "I wish you could have trusted me sooner, but I think I can accept why you didn't," I told him.

He pulled a cloth from his pocket and wiped his eyes. "Michael, I am sorry," he said.

Caroline returned with a bottle of Scotch and two glasses. As I poured, I confessed. "There are a few hard facts about myself I have had to face since this war began. One is that I abhor violence. I must have gotten that from my mother. The second would be the realization that because of number one, I would make a terrible soldier.

"One good thing in all of this mess is I still know how to pick my friends." Holding the glass up, I toasted. "To good friends."

Caroline, carrying a cup of coffee, quietly joined us at the table.

"Knowing these facts, how would you proceed?" I inquired of Stillman.

"Michael, I can't be here anymore, but I would like to stay close. If Miss Jenny would let me slip in at night and stay at her boarding house in an upstairs corner room facing Columbus Street, I could keep an eye on things down here. We can keep the same watch schedule, but I will stay in the shadows most of the time."

I nodded, but he wasn't through.

"I will slip into that shed between the two houses. Remember the bucket in front of the shed? When it's right side up, you know I am close. On dark nights, I will join you between shifts on the porch so we can smoke one of those cigars. I am hoping if we are not seen together, the Rebel Guard will leave you alone.

"During the daytime, you might find me at the Jenny boarding house. If you will continue to trust me with the key, I would like to keep watch from the Customs House. I am hopeful that from there I can find where they hole up during the day. I'll take care of my own provisions, but if you were to leave something from Miss Caroline's kitchen in the shed, it would be nice 'cause I am going to miss her cooking."

Stillman smiled at Caroline as he continued. "I will know after a couple of days what those ruffians are looking for. If you see me, avoid me. If you see another black man hoeing in one of the vegetable gardens here or at the boarding houses, approach him like you are his master. His name is William Marr, and he is another agent working with me here in town."

As he spoke, I looked at Caroline, shrugged, and sighed in disbelief, knowing how blind I had been.

"I've only worked with him for a short time. I believe you can trust him, but he will be safer if you treat him like the help. He will keep an eye on things while you are away during the day and will report to me anything suspicious," said Stillman.

"If these men come at you, do not hesitate—shoot and kill them because I guarantee they will not hesitate to kill you."

I interrupted because I had to know. "How in this world does a black man in the South collect information of any value?"

"Michael, think back into the past, those meetings you held, those social events you attended, and those conversations you had with someone on the street. In all that time, how many black people do you remember? I'm guessing none, but you know as well as I that they were around, attending their masters during those meetings, pouring your drink at a social event, or sometimes just resting, fanning themselves while you talked to friends on the street. We are invisible. The only time most Confederates see us is when we cause trouble."

It was getting late. Stillman bid us farewell for now and walked down the street. He had the first guard, and I knew he would be close.

I was glad when Caroline stayed with me. We talked throughout the night, trying to make sense of it all.

# Chapter XII

## Assassin

Tuesday, April 14, 1863 started like most mornings. Caroline and I walked over, collected Jenny, Ava, and Lottie, and made our way down the street toward the boarding houses.

I saw a figure approaching from several blocks away. The early morning mist obscured all but his outline and revealed a large man. A closer inspection showed bare black feet and tattered clothes. He had on a straw hat with a wide brim that had seen better days. Over his shoulder, he balanced a garden hoe.

The women stopped their discussion as he passed.

I expected him to just tip his hat or give us a wider berth, but to my surprise, he spoke. "Mr. Kohler, Sir. It be all right if I start on the kitchen gardens this mornin'?"

Caught off guard, I hesitated for a moment then responded. "Yes, William, that would be fine."

He tipped his hat. "Thank you, Sir," he said and continued on his way.

I had not expected anything so soon. Lottie, Ava, and Jenny were confounded. I whispered, "I'll explain later." Caroline accompanied Jenny into her boarding house so she would know to leave the one room open and told her not to be fearful if she heard a noise during the day. Lottie and Ava continued to the Florida House to get breakfast started.

After securing the women and checking the rooms, I made my rounds. The Foley house was still locked and boarded up, so I continued to Wefings on the corner of Laurel and Cherry where I received warm greetings and a cup of coffee. From Wefings, I continued down Cherry Street, passed through White Square, and looked left into the Bowery and down Commerce Street toward Blood's Tavern. When I reached the river, I turned right on Water Street and continued on my walk, inspecting the warehouses along the waterfront.

I had both Colt Patersons tucked into my belt and covered with a light coat but found them a poor substitute for Stillman. I missed my friend and felt isolated, paranoid, and exposed. For peace of mind, I occasionally patted my belly, feeling the grips of the guns.

People I knew were beginning to stir and get about their morning's business. I turned right down a narrow alley between two buildings, just before Leslie Street, a shortcut I frequently took over to Commerce Street. As I approached the end of the alley, I felt the ground quake beneath my feet. There was a tremendous crash as bricks and debris began falling at my heels.

Without looking back, I burst out onto Commerce Street, fearful of what might be following. People attracted by the commotion gathered at the opening before the dust cleared.

The third floor wall on the cotton warehouse had collapsed, sending a ton of bricks and mortar crashing to the ground. I knew it was a design flaw that had plagued these warehouses for years, but it didn't lessen my fear or shock at the horror of it all.

I looked upward. "Thank you, God, for saving my life," I said. Most of the warehouses had already been taken down to two stories, but I didn't want to die in the rubble of this one.

Friends and neighbors gathered around.

"You're fortunate to be alive." An elderly woman patted my trembling shoulder.

"I can't believe it," I said. "What a horrible way to die, beneath the crushing weight of those bricks."

From the alley, a voice yelled out. A man gazing from the street turned to relay the alarm. "Somebody get Doc Chapman."

A fire line formed moving the debris into piles on the street.

Doctor Chapman came running. Setting me down on a bench, Dr. Chapman checked me over while the men continued to clear the alley.

"You all right son?"

"Yeah, it all came down behind me. I wasn't hit, thank the Lord."

With the bricks and lumber cleared, men started to leave the alley, opening a path for Doctor Chapman. It was not long before he emerged. Pointing a finger, he told one of the boys: "James run down and get Mr. Tutwiler, the undertaker, and tell him to bring his wagon."

Turning to the men, he told them: "Good job boys, but I'm afraid he didn't stand a chance. You might just as well get him out of there for Mr. Tutwiler." Some of the men passed back into the alley and a minute later emerged with a body.

Doctor Chapman leaned over the body, examining the man's bloody face.

"I don't know this man. Anybody here know this man?" He asked. One by one, the people filed by, but no one knew the identity of the dead stranger.

I walked over and looked at the body. "Afraid I'm no help either Doc. I've never seen him before." As I spoke to Chapman, a man appeared from the alley, dusting off a leather hat. He stooped and placed it over the bloodied face of the dead man.

I felt as though I had been struck by God's own lightning when I saw an owl feather sticking out of the hatband. With a thud, the man dropped a large Bowie knife beside the body. "Don't understand why a man would draw a knife on a brick wall. You know who's gonna win that fight."

Caroline came running down the street. She hugged me. "Are you all right?" She asked. After a quick check, head to toe, she sighed. "You're fine." I calmed her and sat with her on the bench, watching as the men lifted the body into the back of Tutwiler's wagon. The crowd finally disbursed, and Caroline and I walked toward the Florida House.

I inspected the adjacent buildings. Two buildings away from the collapse, in a second floor window, a figure appeared. The figure moved forward out of the shadows and stopped, standing in the shaded light, just shy of the sun. Dead in my tracks, I stared at the apparition.

Caroline glanced at me and directed her gaze at the same window.

I reached under my coat and squeezed the grip of my Colts. The man in the window slowly raised his head and under the brim of his hat was the face of Stillman. He raised his hand, tipped the brim, and disappeared back into the shadows.

Caroline held my arm. "What is that all about?"

Looking down at Caroline, I smiled. "I think Stillman Smith just saved my life."

I knew the odds of this being a random attack were slim. The evidence clearly pointed to assassination. In the future, I needed to vary my route and start growing a third eye in the back of my head. I was lucky today. Stillman had my back. Caroline had almost become a widow before she became a bride.

The night of the fourteenth and the early hours of Wednesday the fifteenth were painfully quiet. Seeing the bucket by the shed turned up, I knew Stillman was in the shadows. Caroline left some stew and cornbread for his supper, and I left some whiskey to take the edge off a long night.

I sat on the porch, watching the houses, but Stillman never made an appearance. The day of the fifteenth was uneventful. William Marr arrived early and was hoeing in the garden when we left. After dropping the women off, I made rounds but dramatically changed my path, sticking to main streets to confuse anyone who might be watching.

My paranoia was at its peak, and it seemed as though I was looking back as much as forward. It was still cool enough to warrant the light coat that covered the grips of my pistols. I wished the Rebel Guard would make their move and get it over with. This waiting and the dreadful feeling of helplessness was hard to bear.

I was pleased the night of the fifteenth when just before midnight, Stillman came in the shadows and spoke with me on the porch.

"How are you holding up, Michael?" he asked.

My response was easy. "Well, I got the Rebel Guard up my ass, and I'm getting married on Saturday. You tell me what is worse, facing all those people at a wedding or the Rebel Guard? I don't see why we couldn't just be married by the Justice of the Peace."

"Don't worry; when you go home on Saturday afternoon with your new bride, it will have been worth facing all those people," Stillman assured me.

"Friend, it's good to see you. I've worried about you more than you could know. I want to thank you for what you did for me. I'd be dead right now if it weren't for you," I told him.

"That was nothing. That wall was about ready to fall anyway; it didn't take much to push it over. Besides, I only meant to push out a few bricks. When that whole damn wall came tumbling down, I was afraid I might have killed you too. I didn't have time to check on your condition. I was moving fast to get out of there before the roof collapsed on my head. You can't know how relieved I was when I saw you and Caroline standing in the street."

That made me smile.

"Listen, you have to stay alert the rest of the night. I got a problem with Marr I need to deal with, so I won't be back until tomorrow night."

We shared a final drink, and Stillman disappeared into the darkness.

The rest of early morning was quiet except three o'clock a.m. when Doc Chapman and Mr. Homer Goodlett passed with lanterns. Doc was going to deliver Goodlett's sixth child. The light and sound from their passing served well to keep me alert.

As a precaution, I changed our departure time, waiting until the sun rose completely before I walked the women to work. No sign of Marr this morning, and when we arrived at the Jenny boarding house, there was no sign that Stillman had been there that night.

I began to worry. I decided to take a chance and walk down to the Customs House to look around. I figured I hadn't been seen there for some time, and it shouldn't raise any suspicions.

I walked slowly toward the Customs House. When the streets were clear, I slipped inside. I had to unlock the door, a good sign, I thought. Tightly gripping both revolvers, I checked around the first floor. The shutters latched from the inside, and showed no sign of forcible entry. I cautiously climbed the stairs to the second floor, stopping and listening every few steps. The light entering through the louvers was bright enough for me to walk about, but it cast eerie shadows.

The door to the larder was closed but unlocked, raising a suspicion in my mind. I walked into the larder and began checking the crates. Everything seemed fine until I got to the crate containing the meat. The lid was off to one side. Inspection showed that two hams and a slab of bacon were missing. Stillman was above suspicion, but I was starting to worry about the problem he had to address with Marr.

I walked down to the Florida House to share what I had found.

Caroline met me at the door of the restaurant. Grasping my arm, she led me into the boarding house.

"We have a guest waiting."

"Who is it?"

"You'll see soon enough."

Caroline opened the door, and there was Hatch, reclining on the bed. He rose quickly to greet us as we entered the room.

"Michael, I'm here for the wedding. Think you can put up your best man for a couple of days?"

"Sure." Looking at Caroline I inquired, "Did you collect the money for the room?"

Caroline, a little slow to catch onto the humor snapped back "Michael! He'll be our guest."

For the amusement of our guest, I responded with what would be described as a typical married man's reply.

"Yes, dear."

Hatch grinned, but Caroline didn't laugh.

"Aren't you taking a chance being here?" I asked.

"Don't worry. The blockade is undergoing a big inspection. They'll be tied up for a couple of days."

"Any chance they'll be tied up until after the wedding?"

Hatch understood my concern, but it didn't help when he replied, "I wouldn't hold my breath."

"Don't you be getting worry lines over it. Your old friend Hatch has got the Union blockade in his back pocket."

I gave a halfhearted laugh. "Yeah, I look forward to seeing that."

"Before you ask, she's fine and growing like a weed. She's up in the swamp with Miss Charity's people. Miss Charity wanted me to tell you she'd try and have her back in time for the wedding, but if not, you need to go ahead, and in her words, 'Do right by Miss Caroline.'"

"I'm trying my best," I told him.

"I won't be staying with you. Caroline was letting me have a lie-in until you got back. I'll stay over with my parents until the wedding. Oh, by the way, I understand you may have some dealings with the Rebel Guard. I'd watch myself if I were you; they're a nasty piece of work. The Confederate Army used them to collect information, but when they started going outside the law and hurting innocent people to line their own pockets, the Confederates broke contact."

I told Hatch and Caroline of my recent discoveries and concerns.

"I already knew Stillman was an agent for the Union blockade." Hatch added, "What you may not know is he was feeding information back to the Confederates through my channels. He's kept us informed about changes in the blockade. You know what a mess this slavery issue is making of the Southern cause. Lots of Confederate soldiers that never owned a slave are starting to have abolitionist tendencies. Stillman's reason for being in this war is pure and simple: abolish slavery. He is willing to lend a sympathetic ear to either side if it furthers the cause.

"What about Marr?" I asked.

"I don't know anything about him, but I can tell you that if Stillman has the Rebel Guard gunning for him, he would be well advised to go home. I'll check in on you every morning and try to be there for you if things start heating up. Right now, I need to let Mrs. Wefing know her son is still alive."

Hatch started for the door. Suddenly he turned, "One more thing. Do you know a Horace Rutledge?"

"No, never heard of him," I answered.

"Yes, you do," Caroline corrected me.

"I think I'd know if I knew a man named Horace Rutledge."

"You do, and you have known him for years; he's the Vicar," Caroline fired back.

"The Vicar...I guess I thought his name was Vicar," I responded.

"Caroline, do you know of anyone else besides the Vicar named Horace Rutledge?" Hatch asked.

"Why, no; he's the only Rutledge around here. Why?"

"I was up near Columbus a little over a month ago and ran across a friend of mine, Oscar Phillips. He was visiting his parents in Columbus, but he works in records for Governor John Milton in Tallahassee. We got to talking about slavery and plantation owners having the most to lose if the South doesn't win the war."

"Yeah, men like Horace Rutledge," were his words.

"You mean the Vicar in Apalachicola owns a plantation?" I asked.

"Can't be the same fellow. This Rutledge lives in Apalachicola, but I understand he has holdings in Jackson County."

"Why does this Rutledge stand to lose so much?" I asked.

"Oscar says he owns one hundred and twelve slaves. That's why."

"I can't believe that," I exclaimed.

"You can imagine my curiosity too. I made an effort to pass through Tallahassee two weeks later. I inquired at the Capitol and found some interesting information on one Horace Rutledge."

"What?"

"I put it to you. Tell me why a Vicar in Apalachicola who owns thirty acres of useless bottom land in Jackson County, Florida would need one hundred and twelve slaves?"

With no answer from either of us, Hatch left and headed home for a well-deserved furlough.

Caroline shook her finger at me. "You watch yourself, Michael Kohler 'cause you're not gonna get out of marrying me," Caroline scolded. I turned, smiled, walked back, and gave her a kiss.

I left, heading to the Customs House to check the docks and look for clues, trying to justify my suspicions.

# Chapter XIII

## Kidnapped

I walked out onto the dock behind the building. April had finally begun to warm up, and the sun made it hard to rationalize the coat I wore to cover my revolvers. Lost in a daydream, I relived my past and the people and events that comprised my life. Upriver a hundred yards, I could see the dock where Old Hickory had tried to make a dinner of my leg.

Examination of the dock revealed no clues, so I turned and walked back toward shore. As I approached the end of the wood planking, I heard a young voice say, "Quiet, Shhhhh."

Looking over the edge of the dock near shore, I commanded, "You boys come out here and talk to me."

In a hangdog fashion, two local boys came from beneath the dock and stood on the shoreline.

"You boys know me?"

One of the boys looked up. "Yes, Sir. You're Mr. Kohler, Pearl's friend."

"You boys are not in any trouble. When I was young, I spent a lot of time under these docks, fishing and floundering. What I need to know, and I need you to be truthful, were you here under this dock last night?"

The boys looked at each other.

"Yeah, but we didn't have anything to do with it. Our parents told us if we knew what was good for us, we'd stay out of it."

In my best business voice, I told the boys, "Tell you what I'll do fellas. If you tell me what happened here last night, I'll never tell your parents, and I'll give you all the coins I have in my pockets. Do we have an accord?"

Excited, the boys nodded their heads and stated for the record, "Yes, Sir!"

I sat on the edge of the dock as the boys told their tale. The older boy did all of the talking as his younger companion nervously looked on shaking his head in agreement.

"You're right. We fished last night in this very spot. We snuck out 'cause we wanted to fish all night. Long about three o'clock in the mornin', we hear a commotion up on the dock, and they was two niggers, a big one and a tall one, havin' an argument about some meat the big one was carryin' in a bag.

"The tall one, he says, 'you don't got no right to pay your gamblin' debts with Mr. Kohler's meat.'

"The big one, he says, 'He's a rich man; he can afford it better than me; he won't miss it anyhow. Why you worried about it? We win this war, we be goin' home soon enough. To hell what he thinkin'. He's just another lying, white man to my concerns.'

"The two of them were arguing about that bag of meat when all of a sudden a voice from the shore says, 'Look what we got here boys, a couple of Kohler's nigger spies. You boys been sellin' that meat to them Yankees. You know that's treason, and we goin' to have to hang you for it. Let's take these niggers into custody, boys.'

"About then, the big nigger, he jump into the river one way and the tall one he jump in the other way. The big one, he got away, but the tall one, he can't swim, so they just plucked him out of the water and took him along with 'um, and that's the truth of what happened."

"Boys, I want you to think real hard. Did you know the man who took the tall, black man?"

"Yeah, we seen him before down at the docks. He answers to the name of Dray."

"Boys, can you tell me what direction they took when they left here?"

125

"Yes, Sir, Mr. Kohler. They headed up-river along the shoreline."

"You did good," I told the boys. Emptying my pockets I handed them what, for a small boy, was a fortune in coins. "You make sure you split that up, all right?"

"Yes, Sir, Mr. Kohler we will," they called out as they ran down the river bank.

Sickened by the news, I now feared for Stillman's life. I headed back to the Customs House. I needed time to think; I needed to come up with a plan. I struggled with the key. When the door finally opened, I passed through, slamming it behind me and walked down the hall to my old office. By the time I came to my senses and saw the broken shutter, it was too late and everything went black.

***

Judgment day was upon me. My eyes opened onto my own personal hell. My head was throbbing. My left eye was swollen to a slit. I sat upright against a wall, knees against my chest. I tried to move, but my hands and feet were bound under my legs. The lashings were so tight my fingers were cold and numb. They no longer obeyed my command. Dried blood dripped from my swollen eye and nose to coat my bare chest. Again, I tried to move. I stopped when intense pain in my ribs halted my breathing. My bad left knee was bent and burned with white-hot flame. I would have gladly paid a king's ransom for a glass of Dr. Gorrie's bitter brew.

Pushing off from the wall, I sat up. Leaning forward added to the pain in my knee but released the tension on the rope that bound my ankles and wrists. I could feel my heart beating in my hands as the blood returned to my fingers. I was grateful the initial blow had rendered me unconscious and spared me from the agony of the beating that must have followed.

The flickering light of a fire passed through the open slits between the planks of my prison, allowing just enough light to give me a spectral impression of my surroundings. My cell was a small wooden shed with

126

a dirt floor. It appeared to be night. Several hours must have passed since my abduction.

As I sat quietly, the throbbing in my head subsided. The ringing left my ears, and I could hear the muffled sound of men talking. Light from the campfire dimmed and reappeared as several shadows moved around the fire.

Ignoring the pain, I scooted on my haunches toward the door. Built of vertical cypress planks, it had shrunk over the years, and the firelight entered through cracks between the boards. From the voices and movement around the fire, I determined there were three men. With my ear to the crack, I could barely make out the conversation.

"He's dead all right; no doubt about it. It was that Kohler's woman that done it. She come down to Blood's, totin' a pistol, spotted poor old Aldridge, and had the nerve to call him out. She commenced to screaming about that Kohler fella's whereabouts, and before you knew it, Aldridge, drunk as usual, pulled out his gun and shot her. Septin' he just winged her in the arm. When she fell backwards, that gun of hers went off, and I tell you what, the last thing that went through old Aldridge's mind was his left eyeball. It took out the whole back of his head."

"What did Dray do?" another man asked.

"He didn't get there until the party was over. He never liked Aldridge much, and I don't imagine he rightly cared if he was dead or not. City folks started showin' up and took the woman to Doc's place. Dray showed up as they was haulin' Aldridge's body away."

"What did Dray say we supposed to do now?"

"I asked him that very same thing, and he was tellin' me about how he was fixin' to kill these two fellas, on account of them bein' spies, and for them sellin' that salted meat to the Yankees. Well, you ain't gonna believe this, but that little old Prickly Pear, she come running out of the dark and stuck a jackknife in Dray's leg. She was yellin' at the top of her lungs, callin' him a bastard, and tellin' him to leave Mr. Brandon alone."

"Did he kill her?"

"I don't know if she dead or not, but I can tell you, he let out a yell. 'You little bitch!' He backhanded her hard. Said he'd deal with the little

127

bitch and the gun-totin' bitch later. She laid crumpled up on the ground, not movin', when I left. So I don't rightly know if she's dead or not."

"We suppose to kill 'im now?" Asked a third man.

"No. We got to wait for Dray. I don't think he cares who kills that nigger, but I know for a fact, he wants a piece of Kohler. Just set tight. Soon as he digs that jackknife outta his leg, he'll hobble out here, and we'll take care of business soon enough."

With the thought of Dray "hobbling out," the three men laughed and got back to drinking.

I was about to go out of my mind with worry: Caroline shot and Pearl, who must have just arrived in town, lying injured in the street. I sat useless. In Hatch's stories, the hero always found a means of escape, a loose rope, or an ax blade to cut the bonds, but in real life, the bonds remained tight, and there was no sharp object to hasten my escape.

Hatch will have been alerted by now, and I knew he would sacrifice himself before he would allow anyone to touch the women.

The night dragged on. It must have been early in the morning, two or three o'clock, before the sound of Dray's voice sent a chill down my spine.

"Boys, you best be bringin' our guests out. They ain't much night left, and there's a powerful lot we got to do in town when the sun comes up."

I heard a door open and close, the sound of a heavy object being dragged over wooden planks, down stairs, and across bare ground. I assumed it was Stillman. Then the steps drew close as they came for me.

The door opened, and two men with torches entered the room, the third waiting outside with a wooden pole. The man I heard speaking earlier said, "You ready for judgment day, Kohler? Devil's waitin' for you just outside." His friend laughed, finding humor in my misery. They placed a croaker sack over my head and secured it with a rope around my neck. The third man entered and ran the wooden pole under my arms and behind my back. The men picked me up by the pole, dragged me out near the fire, and dropped me to my knees on the ground. One of the men gave me a kick, knocking me onto my side.

I could hear them talking in muttered voices from across the fire. One stayed close and upon command removed the sack from my head.

In front of me, across the fire was Dray, standing with the flames illuminating his hardened and filthy appearance. To my left was Stillman, who gazed at me, but since he was gagged, could offer no words. From what I could see, with my face on the ground, he was tied the same as me, except he was on his knees, with the pole resting behind him on his wrists and ankles.

"Set him up boys," Dray barked out the order. They brought me to my knees.

My heart broke as I examined my friend. If I had earlier felt I was in hell, I now knew hell had been reserved for Stillman. Bone protruded from his right arm, and the fingers of his hand hung mangled. His left leg from the knee down lay on the ground, bent and distorted. The soles of his feet were blistered and burned, revealing muscle and bone. Even with his left hand wrapped in a rag, it was easy to see three fingers had been amputated. He had been beaten around his face. His eyes no longer sat square in their orbits. There was a string tied tightly around the skin of his groin to keep him from bleeding after they emasculated him.

Now I knew why he showed no emotion; he was ready to die. If I had a gun and a single bullet, I would do my friend a service.

With torches in hand, the men took the pole by the ends and dragged Stillman away. Dray turned me around. Taking a fist full of hair, he forced my head back to watch the proceedings. Pilings appeared in the torch light as they dragged him down a dock. The third man led the way, igniting torches tied to the pilings as they moved to the end of the dock. With the area now illuminated, I saw the irony of this place. It was the slaughterhouse.

Dropping Stillman on the dock, they turned their attention to the cargo boom. The men pushed down on the counterweight, raising the boom. A chain attached to the other end emerged from the river. The boom turned, swinging the chain over the dock. Meat hooks hanging from the chain held what remained of two boars. The men used the hogs, chumming the river, to attract predators. Cutting Stillman's legs free and removing the gag from his mouth, they hung him by his wrists from the meat hooks. Pushing down on the counterweight, he rose from the dock. Pivoting the weight, he now hung helplessly over the river.

Dray held me by the hair, pulling me forward. He repeatedly pounded my face into the ground, silent until he spoke in a violent tone. "You seein' this, boy?" Mocking, he continued, "What you think of all this, Mr. Michael Brandon Kohler, Sir?" Gripping my hair tighter, he jerked my head to the side so he could look into my eyes.

"It'll be your turn soon enough." He spoke in a calm, sadistic voice. "I know you ain't no spy; that ain't why you're here. You're here 'cause years ago you made a mistake and defended them worthless folks over there in St. Joseph. Wicked city, built by traitors and thieves, another Sodom and Gomorrah. I'm sure your old man was just like you— worthless. You're about to pay for that beatin' you give me. You gettin' a good picture of what's about to happen to you, Mr. Michael Brandon Kohler, Sir?"

He spit on my face and, as he rose to his feet, pulled me to my knees. He commanded the men to lower the boom. Stillman now hung up to his thighs in the river.

For a moment, it was quiet. I felt nothing. Perhaps, like Stillman, I accepted my fate.

Slowly a large gray form appeared near Stillman. Engulfing his left leg within its jaws, the shark pulled the leg, cutting it from his body. Stillman cried out in German. He slumped, his lifeblood flowing into the river.

The men, celebrating what they had done, turned the boom near the dock and cut the rope, commending the body to the river. For a few seconds, the river roiled with a flurry of activity and then once again became silent.

Dray threw me down. With his boot on the side of my face, he ground me into the dirt. His men cackled and mocked as they approached. Dray moved away from the fire toward the dock and greeted his disciples. In low muttered tones, they discussed my death.

# Chapter XIV

## The Gray Soldier

I closed my eyes tightly to try to clear the dirt and blood. When I reopened my eyes, to my disbelief, a figure stood between my assailants and me.

The fire illuminated the back of the stranger. I could see his long, gray Confederate coat. A wide-brimmed Confederate soldier's hat sat on his head, his tied hair hung to the middle of his back. His shadow cast by the fire alerted Dray to his presence, and the men turned to face him.

"Stranger, you're not vested in this, and you best be movin' along," Dray told him.

The figure remained silent. "Are you deaf boy? I said move along. This is none of your business!" The outsider stood his ground and remained silent.

The man standing to Dray's left spoke up. "Let me take care of this fool." He pulled a gun from his belt. The gun had just cleared the holster when a shotgun blast struck him in the head, picking him up, throwing him to the ground. The stranger cocked the second barrel and again stood silent.

Dray and his men were now confounded. With their torches in hand, they stared at the mutilated face of their companion.

Turning back, Dray pointed at me screaming, "Don't you understand that this man is a spy, and we got to kill him."

The gray soldier motioned with the end of his shotgun. Dray and his men dropped their pistols. Then in a move that made no sense, the soldier lowered the sawed-off shotgun, dropped it to the ground.

"So that's how it is," he said, pointing to the man on the ground. "It was him you was after. Shit, now that he's dead, no harm done. Why don't you join us, and we'll take care of this Yankee trash together."

Standing firm, the Gray soldier opened his coat. I could not see what the torch light revealed, but it clearly distressed Dray and the two men who remained.

The man in gray had the advantage with the fire at his back. Dray strained unsuccessfully to see the face of his judge and stood glaring at the shadowy figure, not once breaking his gaze. In a strangled voice, he commanded the man to his right, "Take him."

Dray's man pulled a large, Bowie knife from his belt and stepped forward. "My pleasure." Slinging the knife wildly, he rushed forward but stopped dead in his tracks just short of his target.

The thrust had to have been sudden and accurate. I never saw the Gray soldier move. Dray's man dropped the knife at the soldier's feet and gripped his throat. Through his fingers passed the blade of a saber. He turned to flee but managed one-step before dropping to his knees. He fell forward, driving the blade through the back of his neck.

Dray and his one remaining man now stood alone, facing the Gray soldier.

I could see fear in Dray's eyes as he searched for a way out. His comrade in arms also saw the fear. Dropping his knife, he turned and ran. Dray, out of his mind with anger, reached down, picked up one of the guns, and shot his own man in the back, screaming, "Traitor. Coward!"

Dray turned back to the Gray soldier with the gun ready to fire. Dray watched as a second shotgun blast separated his wrist from his arm. The hand tight around the grip now flew harmlessly away. Dray dropped to his knees, holding his arm in pain, cursing the Gray soldier.

The Gray soldier dropped the shotgun and walked over to Dray. Opening his coat, he withdrew a club and held it, pointing at Dray's face. Dray's only word was, "Foley."

The King of Clubs! The Gray soldier was my friend Jacob. How I had prayed he would come through the war unscathed. Jacob took the club and struck Dray across his jaw, knocking him unconscious, and leaving his mark on Dray's face.

He turned toward me, the fire illuminating his face. "I think you're the most beautiful man I have ever seen," I told him.

Jacob responded, "You look like hell. Bad night?"

He cut me loose and helped me to my feet. We both hobbled over to Dray who began to moan.

"You're walking crippled like me. What's with that?" I asked.

"Minie ball took out most of my calf. If you can't march, you can't soldier."

"Can't soldier, huh?" Looking around at the carnage, I finished my thought. "No kidding. You could have fooled me."

Jacob released me, and I stood on my own. He reached down, grabbing Dray by the hair and dragged him toward the dock.

"Pick up those revolvers." He told me.

I retrieved the revolvers from the ground, but up until now, I had not noticed they were my father's Patersons. I held one and tucked the other in my belt.

We made our way to the end of the dock. Jacob placed Dray on his knees, facing the river.

"I'm done with all the killing. This is your battle. You decide," Jacob said, looking at me.

Dray began to curse me. He called me a coward and told me how he was going to end me. Jacob snapped Dray's head back by his hair. He reached down into Dray's vest pocket and removed Dray's watch, ripping the watch chain from the button on his vest. Jacob handed me the gold pocket watch.

Confused by Jacob's action, I examined the watch. It seemed familiar. Opening the watch, I held it near the torch for a better look. There was an inscription inside the case. "To my loving husband Brandon. Love always Cora." The bastard that had shot and robbed my dying father now knelt in front of me.

"That's right, Kohler. Your old man, he was too weak to raise his sail. I did him a mercy," spoke Dray.

I felt my mind going dark. The Paterson in my hand raised and pointed at the back of Dray's head. I cocked the hammer and pulled the trigger until the gun would fire no more; then, knowing what I had done, I dropped the Colt into the river.

When Jacob released Dray, the body fell from the dock.

Suddenly, as if ordained from hell, Old Hickory, the devil's harbinger himself, rose from the water, caught Dray in midair, and dragged him below. Overwhelmed by the sight, we both stood breathless.

Minutes later, I could see by the glow on the horizon, the sun was on its way.

I began to speak, but Jacob, knowing my thought, interrupted.

"What just happened stays between you, Dray, and Hickory. Don't debate your role in this affair. He was as evil as they come."

"How did you find me?" I asked.

"Strangest thing. I just walked into town from the old Indian Trail. It was too late to call on anyone, so I headed down to the bowery for a drink. I no sooner walked up to Blood's than this little girl come running up holding her face. I stooped down to see what was wrong. I thought I knew. I asked, 'Who hit you, girl?'"

"I'm fine. You're Mr. Foley ain't yah?" she excitedly asked.

"Yes," I said.

"She then proceeded to tell me her good friend, Mr. Brandon Kohler, was in over his head and needed my help. She's the one that pointed me in your direction."

"Pearl," I said.

"Yeah, that was her name, Pearl."

"Is that when you came to my rescue?" I asked him.

"Oh, hell no, I knew you could handle yourself. I was just mad and lookin' for the guy who hit Pearl," Jacob fired back.

We laughed. I warned Jacob to stop before I broke another rib.

When we calmed down some, I asked, "How did you know about the watch?"

"Michael, I want you to remember. I have always been your friend. I saw your dad's watch that night at Blood's Tavern when I checked to see if Dray was alive."

"Why didn't you tell me?" I asked.

"If you had known, you might have gone back, and I knew Dray would kill you. Then later, Dr. Gorrie confided in me that your father was dying from the fever before he was shot. We agreed with no witnesses to prove that Dray pulled the trigger, it would be best to keep silent. Michael, I am sorry, but I could not afford to lose my best friend."

Interrupted by voices in the distance, we turned to face good or bad, whatever was coming.

Lead by Hatch, locals approached down the trail, carrying axes and pitchforks, searching for the Rebel Guard.

Hatch walked up just as bold as you please.

"You two look like shit. Seen anything of the Rebel Guard?"

Laughing with broken ribs is not a good idea, and you would think the pain would keep you from it. I found out that is not the case. I laughed and hurt at the same time.

Hatch had rallied the locals, and together they went on the defensive and rooted out the rest of the Rebel Guard. Four of the Guard were shot and killed. Two more were being detained, awaiting a hanging.

Hatch looked at Jacob.

"Let's see. I got six, and you got three. I thought you were supposed to be some big scary soldier. What happened to you? You wearin' dresses now?"

I was in pain, laughing, as I limped down the dock. The rivalry between these two friends had picked up right where it left off.

Seeing the bodies of the dead loaded onto a wagon started me thinking of Stillman. I was saddened by the loss of my friend. I felt haunted by the thought of his wife and daughters back in Vermont, waiting for a father who wouldn't return from the war.

My eyes teared up as I remembered his last words, in German: "Remember me to my wife and children." I felt at the time that the words had fallen on the ears of a dead man. Having survived, I would now make it my mission to convey his last thoughts.

Caroline spotted me approaching and came running. Her arm was in a sling, and I could tell by her movement, she was in pain. She cried uncontrollably at first but soon began her assessment of my condition.

We both stopped and stood silently as Jenny—overwrought by the sight of her son—fell to her knees. Holding her hands over her mouth, she wept tears of joy. Jacob pulled his mother to her feet and held her, stroking her hair.

Pearl stole the day when she came running up, yelling in celebration. Her very presence raised the spirits of all who had gathered. Her jaw was bruised and swollen, and her eyes were blackened where that bastard, Dray, struck her.

# Chapter XV

## Family

Caroline insisted on going directly to Doctor Chapman's house. Chapman kept me for two hours, loaded me up on laudanum, and sent me home. I slept until three in the afternoon.

Caroline was in a chair by my bed when I woke up. Lottie later told me she never left my side, watching to make sure I was breathing.

Caroline was also hurt. The bullet had passed through her shoulder, fracturing her shoulder blade. She grimaced in pain at the smallest movement. Riddled with guilt, I felt her pain. If I had just been more cautious at the Customs House, this would not have happened. Broken ribs on both sides hindered my rising from the bed.

Hatch, his father, and Doctor Chapman came in from the kitchen and sat me on a chair.

Chapman wrapped my chest tightly in bandages. He was confident the ribs would heal on their own but alerted us to watch closely for signs of pneumonia.

Out of concern for our well-being and much to Caroline's disappointment, he advised against the wedding. I watched as Caroline listened to his advice. It was all I could bear, knowing she suffered physical injury at the hand of Aldridge. I would not allow her to despair over the wedding.

In a guarded voice, I asked Doctor Chapman, "Doc, you coming to the wedding tomorrow?"

"Yeah, I'll be there. I will bring my bag. I like to stay close to patients who are most in need of my care," he replied.

I looked over at Caroline who was having trouble raising her head.

"Aren't we going to make a fine entrance walking down the aisle tomorrow? With all that has happened, I figure if we can survive tomorrow, we can survive anything."

Caroline, overjoyed at my decision, moved to the door.

"I'm going to have Lottie make us some coffee, and when I get back, I'll bring the Laudanum. We will both take a dose, and then you are going to get up and practice walking. I told you before; you aren't getting out of this ceremony," she said.

"I'm not trying to get out of it. I'm looking forward it." I told her.

"You're a good man, Michael Brandon Kohler."

I made up my mind to carry on for Caroline's sake. I would need to wear my best face for the wedding, but my mind was a different matter. Questions gnawed at me and found their way into my waking dreams. Questions about Pearl, the Vicar, and the man I now despised the most, William Marr.

If only Stillman had taken the Navy Colt to confront Marr; there might have been a much different outcome.

After I left for the docks, Caroline found the revolver under the mattress in Stillman's room at the Jenny boarding house. Perhaps providence played a role in Stillman's decision to leave the gun.

Would Caroline have confronted Aldridge without the gun? I asked myself.

Worst of all, I was having a conflict of conscience over Dray's death. I felt no remorse for being the instrument of his murder, but did this mean I had lowered myself to his level? In the future, if I should confront William Marr, would I once again see nothing but rage and darkness and pull another trigger?

Then a thought gave me some comfort: Perhaps the fact that I was even asking the question is what separated me from men like Dray and Aldridge.

Caroline and I took a painful walk down Columbus Street. We both chuckled when we discovered going up stairs hurt just as bad as going down. On our walk, she told me Pearl had paid a visit early in the morning but couldn't stay. Miss Charity was feeling poorly, and she had no one to watch over her. Pearl's compassion seemed endless. We were saddened, knowing how hard Pearl's life had been and that she had never known a childhood. Yet, it was this same hard life which defined Pearl's character.

Caroline shared with me the conflict she now felt over the death of Aldridge. I told her my thoughts and hoped she might find some comfort in my words. It was good that she could not remember intentionally pulling the trigger; in her mind, the gun had just gone off. She was troubled that some of our neighbors felt that the death of Aldridge was justified and perhaps even ordained. She told them that she alone would face God's judgment and prayed he would be merciful.

I was starting to understand it was a matter of perspective. In all honesty, when I think of that drunkard's bullet ripping through Caroline's shoulder…if there was ever a justifiable shooting, this was it.

Of course, with Caroline, I could never put voice to that opinion. My prayers tonight would be that God would hold me accountable for the death of Aldridge and release Caroline from her burden. Perhaps someday, I would be able to tell her of the gruesome role I played that night on the slaughterhouse dock, but this was not the time.

We returned home. Jenny helped Caroline up the steps at the old home place on Laurel while Lottie and Ava helped me into my bed, at my own home. Lottie slept in the parlor in case I needed something in the night.

It was a long night. I leaned on pillows to keep fluid from settling in my lungs. Most of the time, I sat on the edge of the bed with my head in my hands. What little sleep I got came from a bottle of Laudanum. Lamplight from windows at the house next door told me Caroline might also be having a rough night.

I couldn't help but hear the hurried steps as Lottie, Ava, and Jenny ran back and forth between houses. I assumed they were putting the final touches on preparations for the wedding. We were fortunate to have such devoted friends.

I heard the mantle clock chime three-thirty a.m. but didn't hear it again until the clock struck five a.m. All was now quiet. Today was my wedding day, yet my body ached all over.

Doctor Chapman came at six thirty to check on my progress. He helped me up to put on my robe. Lottie delivered breakfast at seven o'clock. Having seen Doctor Chapman's carriage, Lottie brought enough for two. I insisted Doctor Chapman join me for coffee and breakfast. His next stop was to check on my bride's condition.

Hatch arrived at eight o'clock. Between the two of us, we succeeded in stuffing my broken body into a suit. It hadn't occurred to me that my white shirt would not fit over the bandages binding my chest.

"According to your girth, Caroline must be an exceptional cook," Hatch remarked.

"It's the bandages," I replied.

"So Caroline is not a good cook. Is that what you're saying?" Hatch asked.

"No. That's not what I am saying." In the mirror, I noticed my belly bulging out from under the bandages. "Okay. You may have a point. It could be a combination of bandages and food."

"You should confess; you're turning into a regular blow fish," Hatch chuckled.

"Would you please just concentrate on getting my shirt buttoned?" Hatch examined the situation carefully and suggested that since I was wearing a waistcoat, he could split my shirt in the back and we could button the front.

"You'll look good from the front and as long as you leave your coat on, no one will be the wiser," he assured me.

"Fine. Just get it done." Cutting the shirt in the back allowed us enough fabric to button it over my belly in front, and the waistcoat covered the slit in the back.

Hatch held my pants up. "There is no way these pants are going over that big blow fish butt of yours. No offense, but you could push away from the table occasionally. The ass I'm lookin' at now is bigger than the one I looked at pulling the wagon over here."

He was right about the shirt, so I figured there was no need to argue. He was probably right about the butt too, I thought. We tried anyway, but there was no way my pants where going to fit.

I sent Hatch to fetch a pair of my father's black pants from the wardrobe. I intended to have them altered to my size years ago but never got around to it. The pants didn't match the dark blue waistcoat but would have to do in a pinch. They were two inches too long but Hatch did a fair job of pining them up. They were tight in the waist, and we were barely able to button them. I was ready to go.

Hatch helped me out into the hall, but as I took the first step down the stairs, the middle button on my fly gave way and shot off to regions unknown. I couldn't bend over to see the damage, but I felt the draft.

"Hatch, you got any suggestions?" I asked.

"Yeah. I can fix this," he said.

He headed back into the bedroom and soon returned, pulling his jackknife from his pocket. After a few moments, the draft stopped, and I was down the stairs.

"How'd you fix that?" I asked.

"Cut a little hole where the button was and tied it with a string."

"Good man. There might be hope for you yet."

At nine o'clock, we headed out the door for the church. I had seen a carriage pull up to the Laurel house to transport the women. However, the wagon Hatch acquired did not come with a winch and boom. As I raised my leg to the wagon step, there was the unmistakable sound of a seam giving way, followed by a tremendous draft. I ripped the crotch of my pants.

"Hatch, what the hell am I going to do now?"

"I can fix this." Hatch ran back into the house. Moments later, he came running out carrying a piece of black fabric. He put it over and under my belt in back and brought it between my legs to mask the hole in my crotch.

"There, it's fixed. You can't even tell. The colors match perfect."

"Thank God for good friends. Thanks Hatch." I then sucked in my ample gut so he could refasten my pants.

There was no way I was getting in that wagon, so we began walking the four blocks to the church.

"This is a good thing. You smell a little stale, so the walk will be a good way to air you out a bit," Hatch told me.

Somewhat amused by his remark, I rolled my eyes, shook my head, and smiled. "You flap-jawed, barnacle head."

Two blocks into our walk, I felt a bit more limber.

"Hey gimpy. What happened to your limp?" asked Hatch.

I was concentrating on the pain in my ribs and didn't noticed that my bad knee was bending and my gait was dramatically improved.

"How do you like that? Look at me strolling along."

I'd never thought the injuries I sustained at the hands of the Rebel Guard would have an unseen benefit. Feeling a little spry, I increased my pace.

Dr. Chapman met us in the churchyard and removed the bandage covering my eye.

"The swelling has reduced," he said. "Not too hideous. What do you think Wefing? Leave it on or take it off?"

Hatch, being Hatch, said, "No, no, that's not swelling. He always looked that way." Dr. Chapman cackled and Hatch grinned.

"Would you like to move the ceremony to a more appropriate place, perhaps the surgery at my house?" asked Dr. Chapman. Hatch chuckled.

Chapman stood back and looked me over head to toe. "That's a little bold. Do you really consider it that much of a gift?" Chapman remarked.

"What are you talking about?" I asked.

"I know every man thinks he's special, but to put a pink bow on it at your wedding seems a little overboard," Chapman said. Hatch remained noticeably quiet.

"What are you talking about, Doc?" I asked.

"You have a little pink ribbon tied in a bow holding your fly shut. That's what I'm talking about." Chapman smiled.

"Hatch, you idiot. What were you thinking?"

"It's the only thing I could find," he said.

Chapman had an idea. He brought a Bible from the church and cut off the black ribbon used to mark the pages. He changed the pink ribbon to black.

"There; that's better," he announced.

\*\*\*

I made my way up to the altar and stood slightly bent, as Caroline, Jenny, Lottie, and Ava entered from the side of the pulpit. Caroline wriggled her shoulder as if trying to find a way to minimize the pain. She stood tall in her wispy, floral-print gown. She looked at me with a happy, though befuddled look.

I could see the results of the labor of the women in Caroline's wedding garb. The wedding gown fit her tall, slender body perfectly. Her gauzy veil was attached to a ring of yellow daisies. She held a bouquet of daisies. I swear the daisies in that bouquet winked at me.

I squared my shoulders. I must have been the proudest man on earth at that moment. The look she gave me would have melted stone.

I found out later, she told the Vicar to keep it brief; she didn't want me passing out.

We made it through the ceremony without incident, but as we walked down the aisle past our friends and neighbors, they started laughing. The seam in the seat of my pants opened, and the fabric Hatch selected became apparent. To all gathered, peeking out from the seat of my pants, in splendid golden thread, was the all-seeing-eye of the Masonic Lodge. If I lived to be a thousand, I would never live this down.

The reception was set up in City Square, and it looked as though the entire town had shown up for the celebration. I emptied the larder, and the women set the tables with plates of food fit for a king. I forgave Hatch when I saw his gifts of hard-to-acquire delicacies spread across three tables.

We were just seated when the alarm went up. Union whaleboats landed at the docks. Jenny held Jacob back and sent him into the church out of sight. We watched as twenty, heavily armed men in quick march came down Center Street. They stopped just short of the gathered crowd.

William Budd, Commander of the U.S. Naval Force blockading Saint George Sound led the procession. He stood at full attention and announced:

"Be informed that an inquiry will be made into the disappearance and whereabouts of two citizens of Apalachicola, one Stillman Smith and his companion William Marr. Would anyone present know the whereabouts of these two men?" The silence was deafening. My heart stopped at the mention of Stillman's name.

Suddenly Hatch stepped forward. Everyone listened intently, waiting, anticipating what he was about to say.

Hatch acknowledged the commander's authority by slightly bowing his head. "Yes, commander. I'm sure I speak for all gathered when I say we appreciate your concern over our missing citizens, and I am sure by Monday we might be able to help you in your investigation." Once again, he slightly bowed his head to the commander and cast his gaze toward a wagon parked along Broad Street. Smiling, he gazed back at the commander.

"Seize that wagon," the commander ordered. His men rushed toward the wagon. Then he announced, "I am commandeering this wagon and will return Monday to start a full investigation into the Marr and Smith affair."

The Union commander started to leave, then turned and gave me the Masonic handshake. "Brother, you appear to have some odd Masonic rites here in the South." He and his troops walked back toward their boats, the wagon in tow. I noticed the mayor standing with his mouth gaping open in disbelief.

Looking at Hatch, all I could think to say was, "What the hell was that?"

Caroline slapped my arm, pointing at the Vicar standing at the end of the table.

"Hatch," I said.

"Yes, Michael," he answered.

"What the hell was in that wagon?" Once again, I received a warning poke from Caroline.

"Michael, you remember those crates I left you at the Narrows?"

"Yes, Hatch, I do."

"Compared to the crates in that wagon, your crates were full of hardtack and rancid meat." A smile came over his face.

"Hatch, did you just bribe the Union Navy?"

"Yes, Michael. I told you I had the Union blockade in my back pocket. It was you who didn't believe your old friend Hatch."

At this point, I shut my mouth and sat down beside Caroline. The festivities began, I didn't want to look at him because I knew he would have that sly, smug, grin on his face.

Owing to Hatch, I was now humiliated in both the North and the South. I reminded myself that his intent was pure. Many times over the years, I had thought of feeding him to Old Hickory, but somehow he always managed to redeem himself.

Only a king could have afforded the delectable repast. My mouth watered. When the last person was seated, we rose yet again, and the Vicar blessed the food. The longest blessing in history.

Ham, wild turkey, oyster stew, fried river catfish, large baked redfish, oyster dressing, salads, vegetables, breads, and a huge bowl of chicken and dumplings filled the table. Caroline passed the bowl along to me.

"You don't like dumplings?" I asked.

"I do," answered Caroline, "but that was Miss Purdy."

"Miss Purdy?"

"One of my hens. She was a bit past her prime—just an egg every other day, but she had been my lap hen." Caroline replied.

"Lap hen?"

"I used to let the ladies out in the morning. I loved to sit and watch them scratch, but Miss Purdy would hop on my lap, sit quietly, and lay her egg. Why couldn't it have been Hortense? She's my best layer, but a more hateful bird, I haven't known. I'd have no qualms wringing that bird's scrawny neck."

I raised my eyebrows; there were tears in her eyes. What this woman has sacrificed for me. I felt humble...and a bit confused. Was it better to be a beloved bird like Miss Purdy or alive like Hortense? No matter what, in the future, I would try to remain productive.

Just across the way, a long table of desserts followed a table of drinks although the men seemed to be obtaining libation from a carriage parked nearer to the horseshoe game.

With the celebration under way, Caroline and I shared a concern, Pearl's absence. We knew Miss Charity must be in a bad way.

\*\*\*

At five o'clock, the reception wound down. A few celebrants remained, laughing and frolicking. It was well worth the pain and discomfort. I sat down to rest. Hatch was still discoursing on the futility of war. Caroline sat beside me.

Lottie appeared and led Caroline behind the church. A few moments later Caroline signaled to me.

When I arrived, Caroline was trying to console a weeping Pearl. Pearl hugged me and held on as I sat down beside her. In a bittersweet voice, she told us Miss Charity had died. The closest thing to a mother Pearl knew passed away.

"Miss Caroline, Mr. Brandon, I don't know what I'm gonna do. Miss Charity is gone to see Jesus, and my Papa hasn't come home. I got no place to go." I couldn't look at Caroline because I knew she was crying.

"Don't you worry Pearl," I reassured her. "Me and everybody else will find your Papa. I need you to be brave. If I remember right from Miss Charity, she said your Papa's name was Guillaume Gauthier Verheist, is that right?"

Pearl nodded her head. "But they don't call him that. It's too hard to remember. They just call him Dray 'cause that what he does for a livin'. He's a drayman down at the wharfs."

My heart stopped beating, and the blood rushed from my head. I turned away and fell from the bench on all fours. I rested my head on the ground, trying to recover. What had I done?

Pearl of all people laid her hand on my back to comfort me. "Are you all right Mr. Brandon? I'm right here and won't leave you until you're better. Please be all right, Mr. Brandon."

When I recovered, Pearl helped me back onto the bench.

"Until we find your father, you're going to stay with me and Miss Caroline," I told Pearl. She looked up at Caroline. Caroline nodded her head in approval as Pearl embraced her.

***

It had been a trying day for all of us. We left the gathering and walked home. Caroline made hot tea with honey, and we sat in the front room.

Pearl told us she wasn't worried about Miss Charity. "Miss Charity said Jesus was callin' her home to live with him, and that is just where she needed to be. She said she'd miss me a powerful lot, but she'd be watching over me from Heaven."

"Pearl, Miss Charity told me you've got charms you hand out to people that help them through bad times. How come you never gave me and Miss Caroline one of your charms?"

"Why Mr. Brandon, you just gone and answered your own question. You got me, Miss Caroline, and Mr. Hatch, and so many friends, I can't even count all of 'em. You and Miss Caroline don't need any charms."

"Well, tell me how is it you pass out all them charms to folks, and we never heard about it till now?" I asked her.

Pearl looked thoughtful.

"Man in the Bible once said, don't store up treasure down here, keep 'em in heaven, and the Vicar told me the best way to do that is to be 'nonymous when you give things. Otherwise they only counts down here."

We sat, thoughtfully, and sipped our tea. Pearl stood up. "I'm worn out. Is it okay if I go on to bed?" She yawned and walked toward the stairs.

"Sure sweetheart," said Caroline.

"I need to know one more thing before you go. Is telling me these things going to put those heavenly treasures at risk?" I called out.

Pearl stopped and sat on a step, looking at us through balusters. She picked her words carefully.

"No, Mr. Brandon. The Vicar says that a child got to honor certain people, and if they ask questions, a child got to answer truthful. I ain't never had what you'd call a real family, so I kinda made one up in my head. Since then, I been tryin' to put one together for real. I don't mean to make you and Miss Caroline upset by tellin' you this, but I don't think I can lose those treasures by tellin' my father and mother...even if it is the family I just made up in my head."

Pearl walked up the stairs. I didn't dare turn and face Caroline. There were feelings welling up in me, making it hard to swallow. I knew if I looked at Caroline and saw the same, I would not be able to control what I was feeling. We sat in silence, rubbing our eyes and trying to breathe.

Some of what Miss Charity said now made sense. The big question I asked in my mind was "Who is this child?"

# Chapter XVI

## Miss Pearl and her Charms Mean Freedom

Pearl was up early, helping Lottie in the kitchen. Ava and Jenny would have to care for the guests at the boarding houses on their own this morning. Although Caroline said the pain was no longer so sharp, she still relied on Lottie to help her dress and prepare for the day. Lottie had been Caroline's rock since the death of her first husband.

I awoke stiff and sore but felt rather pleased with myself as I looked over at Caroline lying beside me. Alone for so many years, I had a companion with whom to share my life. Never speaking of it, my mother had worried about her awkward son. She would have approved of Caroline and reveled in our union.

Pearl was right in the thick of things, and, little did I know, she decided to take over responsibility for my well-being.

I responded to a gentle tap at the door. "Who is it?"

"Me, Mr. Brandon," a voice whispered.

"Well, you better come in."

Sitting beside me on the edge of the bed she whispered, "Is Miss Caroline awake?"

Caroline moved to prop herself up. "I'm awake sweetheart. How did you sleep last night?"

"Just fine. I went to sleep thinking good thoughts. Miss Charity always told me if you do that, you'll have good dreams."

Pearl sat up closer beside me and leaned on my side. Even with pain still throbbing in my ribs, I put my arm around her. I glanced over at Caroline. She took one look at my face.

"Looking very smug this morning, Mr. Kohler."

"I'm feeling very smug today, Mrs. Kohler."

Embracing Pearl I asked, "What do you think about living here with us?"

She looked up at me and over at Caroline who nodded her head in approval.

"I think that would be the most wonderful thing ever," said Pearl. "Matter of fact, I think it's me feelin' a little smug this morning," she smiled ear to ear.

Caroline was in tears when Pearl got up and moved to the end of the bed. She wanted to know if she could ask a question.

"Of course," Caroline assured her.

Pearl chose her words carefully.

"Miss Charity told me this might happen. She was almost sure of it and told me not to be shy. 'Pearl you got to be bold,' she told me. That means brave."

She took a deep breath. "So I'm just gonna come right out and ask you; would you and Mr. Brandon care much if I were to call you Mother and Father?"

A catch in my rib slowed me down, and Caroline beat me to the hug that followed. I looked at Pearl now in Caroline's arms.

"I think that would be the most wonderful thing ever," I said. We all sat in bed feeling smug about ourselves.

\*\*\*

Lottie had breakfast ready. "Would it be okay if me and my Aunt Lottie bring the breakfast?" Pearl asked.

I nodded yes. From the kitchen, I heard Pearl ask Lottie, "Have you met Uncle Jacob? He's real nice. I think you'd like him."

After breakfast, we dressed and strolled to church. Jacob attended with his mother Jenny proudly on his arm. Hatch arrived with his parents.

Everyone sat in their traditional family pews, reserved since before the war began.

Pearl chuckled when after the service, Caroline asked if I had heard a word of the Vicar's sermon, or had I slept through the entire service.

"Every word," I responded.

"Tell me then. What did he talk about?"

"Sin."

"What did he say about it?"

"He's against it." I took her arm, and we walked home.

***

After dinner, we sat on the porch. I looked forward to a long afternoon of warming my bones in the late April sun.

Pearl sat on the top porch step. She turned her attention to me.

"Father," she said. "We should get ready to go."

"Go where?"

"Uncle Jacob and Uncle Hatch will be here soon with the mule, and we have to get the wagon ready."

"Ready for what?"

"To go over and get my things at Miss Charity's, so I can move in proper."

Caroline smiled. She gave me a look she would use many times in the future when she wanted me to do her bidding.

"Of course, we need to go and get your things." I rubbed my chin; my ribs still hurt.

Pearl ran inside to get her shoes.

"It's the right thing to do," said Caroline. "With her father and Charity gone, she needs a place she feels secure. It's important that a woman has her things about her. However, I do have to say she is one independent child. You can tell by the way she takes charge; she's been running her life since she could walk."

"Who are we kidding? She arranged to have Uncle Jacob and Uncle Hatch come over on a Sunday afternoon to move her things. It's not just her life she's running."

151

As we spoke, Pearl burst from the door, waving as Hatch and Jacob approached with a mule in tow. We hitched the wagon and climbed in. Pearl and I drove the mule, mostly Pearl. Hatch and Jacob followed up the procession by sitting on the back of the wagon.

I knew things would work out. It wouldn't take long to break down an old wardrobe and pick up a few dresses. Then I could return to my porch and bake in the April sun as planned.

It was just a short ride down High Street to the Orman House. When we arrived, Miss Sadie Orman, Thomas Orman's granddaughter, greeted us. Pearl climbed off the wagon and gave Miss Sadie a hug. Miss Sadie stroked Pearl's cheek and consoled her over the loss of Miss Charity. Sadie asked if we needed help moving the wardrobe. I pointed to Hatch and Jacob and told her Pearl had brought her own crew. Sadie, amused by the statement, understood all too well who the boss of this crew was.

"Miss Charity left everything to Pearl," Sadie told us. "Please feel free to take anything you want from the cabin. I know how much Miss Charity meant to her."

Hatch lifted my father's toolbox from the wagon, and we proceeded to the slave shack. I had never seen the wardrobe until now. The three of us stood dwarfed in the enormity of its presence. It stood all of nine feet high and five feet across, with a depth of near three feet. We stared at it. I could see this small project had just grown into a day's work.

Pearl was outside talking to Miss Sadie.

"What have you gotten us into?" asked Hatch.

"Me," I announced. "Don't blame me. Think back to who arranged this. By the way, who paid for the mule?"

"Pearl gave me the money. I figured it came from you," said Jacob.

"Not my money; maybe Caroline's. We may as well get started tearing this beast apart."

That very moment, Pearl rushed in and flung open the doors of the wardrobe.

"You couldn't fit a flea in there," said Jacob in amazement.

Pearl began unpacking the wardrobe onto the floor, letting us know we could load the pieces of the box first and lay her dresses on top. With the wardrobe empty, Hatch stood inside the cabinet and drove the wooden wedges out of their slots to release the top. The one time my height would have been of use, but because of my ribs, I couldn't get my arms above my shoulders. I looked at Hatch and Jacob and shrugged. "Sorry boys."

Somehow they managed to remove the top using a couple of boards from outside. We slipped the pins on the hinges and removed the doors. Wedges held the sides and back in place. The remainder of the wardrobe came apart easily.

We carried the parts out and stacked them by the wagon. The base was all that remained. Although it was larger than the heavy top, Jacob and Hatch felt confident they could lift and load it into the wagon.

Standing at both ends, they lifted from the wedges inside the top of the base, but the heavy platform didn't budge. They checked to see if it might be nailed to the floor, but it wasn't. They tried to pry it away from the wall, but it wouldn't shift.

Pearl was arranging her dresses on a small table out on the porch. When she heard a critical comment from Hatch, she came running.

"Oh, my, you're almost finished. All we have to do now is get my charms, and we can go home," she said.

We all looked at Pearl, confused, having no idea what she was talking about—until she began removing the boards from the top of the platform.

We all thought the bottom of the wardrobe was hollow. Staring, Jacob, was unable to alter his gaze and began rubbing his head. Hatch fell to his knees with his hands resting on the edge, and was for the first time in his life, speechless. I couldn't comprehend if what I was seeing was real.

"This is the same way the Vicar acted when I showed him my charms," Pearl said.

Hatch strained to pick up one of the bars of gold bullion, neatly stacked in the hollow.

"This is Pirate Henry Morgan's Spanish gold, fifteen and sixteen hundreds," Hatch exclaimed.

"Pearl, are these your charms?" I asked.

Pearl smiled and held my hand.

"Yes, Father…some of them anyway."

It was the first time she had called me father in front of others. She couldn't have cared less about the gold and instead gazed at me. I could see in her eyes what Miss Charity had known all along. I remembered Charity's words to Caroline, "I know down deep in my soul this child has been special blessed by God himself."

God's greatest gift, grace, freely flowed in Pearl and was now spilling out to me. Pearl's treasures were the people who surrounded and loved her. To her, words like father and family were more precious than gold.

"Father, Uncle Hatch, Uncle Jacob, let's get this loaded into the wagon. I want to go home and work on my room." Pearl rushed back out onto the porch and finished folding her dresses.

Discussion was brief. We would load now and talk about this later in a more secure place.

We moved the panels of the wardrobe over to the street side of the shack and pulled the wagon to this more secluded side of the building. Like thieves in the night, we passed the gold bars through the side window and layered them into the bottom of the wagon. There were three different sizes of gold bars stowed in the bottom of the wardrobe, enough to cover the bed of the wagon.

The wardrobe emptied of its treasure, Pearl walked over to inspect the job. "Almost done," said Pearl, and she reached into the platform and began removing floorboards from inside. In disbelief, we gazed into a compartment that had been built into the floor beneath the wardrobe. The secret compartment held an equal amount of bullion.

Hatch and Jacob moved the platform out to the wagon, and we loaded a second layer of gold into the wagon bed. Finally finished, we covered the gold bullion with the panels from the wardrobe and finished off the wagon load with Pearl's personal effects.

Secured, we were ready to travel, but Pearl disappeared.

A few moments later, we heard something being dragged. We looked out to see Pearl pulling a ladder from Orman's mule barn toward the shack.

"I think we're ready to go," I told Pearl.

154

"Would it be all right if I get my jewelry first?"

"Yes. We can get your jewelry before we go."

"Up there, Uncle Jacob," she pointed to a small panel in the ceiling at the center of the room.

Jacob pushed the panel up with the leg of the ladder and climbed up, sticking his head into the attic space.

"They're in those two bags." Jacob started to hand a heavy, woven, medium-sized sack down to Hatch. We froze in our tracks when we heard voices from behind the shack.

Shielded by the wagon from the street, I slowly leaned out the side window to look past the brick chimney.

"Union," I turned back into the room.

Jacob disappeared into the attic space, returning the panel to cover his hiding place. Hatch removed the ladder and carried it to the porch.

"I want you to stay here with Uncle Hatch while I see what's going on," I told Pearl.

"Yes, Father," she replied.

I circled left around the shack on the opposite side from the wagon. Having seen the troops approaching, Sadie and her grandfather Thomas Orman approached down the drive from the house.

Thomas Orman inquired boldly, sarcastically, "To what do we owe the pleasure of your company on a Sunday?"

"Are you one Thomas Orman of Apalachicola?" replied the officer in command of the Union troops.

"Yes."

The commander motioned to his men, and they began to surround Orman and Sadie, guns at the ready. "Please be informed you are under arrest, charged as a conspirator in the disappearance of one Stillman Smith and William Marr, citizens of Apalachicola."

My heart sank as I heard Stillman's name. They led Orman away, holding him on the street. The commander in charge informed Sadie they would return Monday to discuss the arrest. He then turned his attentions to me, motioning his men toward the wagon. "Please identify yourself and your business here today?"

"Michael Kohler," I said, feeling like a rat in a trap.

155

Before I could state my business, Pearl came from around the chimney, startling the troops. They readied their guns and pointed them at her. She was the only thing standing between the Union blockaders and the wagon.

"Hello." Pearl smiled at the soldiers.

Disconcerted, they looked back to the commander for orders.

"Lower your guns," he yelled.

Pearl continued past them and took my hand.

"Father, I have all of my things loaded in the wagon. Can we go home now?"

"That is up to the commander," I told her.

He stooped down. "What are you doing here today young Miss?" He asked Pearl.

Pearl smiled. "I was an orphan till Mr. Kohler and Miss Caroline told me they wanted to be my new mother and father. Father came with me to get my wardrobe and dresses. I'm going to have a room of my own."

The commander stood and signaled his men to stand down. They left, marching down the street with Orman in custody.

When the patrol was out of sight, Pearl and I walked back into the cabin to check on the uncles. Hatch was pale as a ghost and helping Jacob down the ladder with the second of two, heavy, canvas bags.

"You two all right?" I asked.

"I am, but I think Jacob may need to change his pants," said Hatch. We all laughed nervously, not believing what we just got away with.

"What's in the bags?" I asked Pearl.

"My jewelry. Miss Charity said they was jewelry filled with what she called diamonds and rubies and rocks like that," she laughed.

"There's even strings of pearls in there, not like me though. The ones that come out of oysters. I even have a crown so sometime me and Miss Charity played a game like I was the queen of Apalachicola. I'd wear my best dress and dance around the room wearin' my crown."

Shaking their heads, Hatch and Jacob walked away, dumbfounded by the tale.

We headed out the door to the wagon. It would be a long, slow trip home. The wagon, grossly overloaded, creaked and sagged under the weight. The axles bowed, and the tops of the wheels tilted in toward the load. The wheels left ruts in the soft ground. I led the mule as it strained to move the wagon. Hatch and Jacob each grabbed a wheel, helping the poor animal, until the wagon moved onto the harder street bed.

We all walked alongside as Jacob led the mule down the street. The sun was setting, and except for the lantern light, darkness concealed our movements.

We breathed a sigh of relief as the wagon came to rest beside the house. Hatch unhooked the mule and led him away. We all smiled, knowing we were home free. Just at that moment, the back axle shattered, and the rear of the wagon came crashing to the ground. Looking at the damage, I was thankful the box held and the load, now at a precarious angle, stayed in place.

Caroline came out of the house alarmed by the noise. Pearl ran up the steps, assured her everything was fine, and greeted her with a hug, telling Caroline how much she had missed her.

"The Vicar is here for a visit; you boys come on inside. Coffee's ready. We've been waiting supper for you," said Caroline.

Bursting with news, we held our tongues as we sat at the table chatting with the Vicar. After supper, we retired to the parlor for conversation. Caroline excused Pearl who went out onto the porch. For the first few minutes, we discussed the weather. I was telling the Vicar of Orman's arrest by the Union blockaders when Pearl came through the door.

Pearl entered the house backwards, bent over, bumping the door open with her bottom. Caroline and the Vicar watched as she strained to pull a heavy canvas sack toward the stairway. She then proceeded to pull and bump the bag up each step, occasionally resting and smiling at Caroline and the Vicar though the balusters. Hatch, Jacob, and I continued the conversation as though nothing was unusual.

After Pearl disappeared into her room, Caroline turned to me with a look. I never understood how with just a look she could ask a question and elicit a response from me.

The Vicar saved me when he asked, "Pearl's jewelry?"

"Yes," I answered. "You know don't you?"

"Yes, and now that I know you know, I think we'd better have a conversation."

Caroline looked from one to the other. "Will someone tell me what's going on?"

I asked Caroline if she might check on Pearl and put her to bed before I attempted to explain. She walked up the stairs into Pearl's room. A few minutes passed before she quietly returned and sat beside me on the sofa. Around her neck, she wore a rather large Spanish gold and emerald pendant on a gold chain.

Caroline, staring blindly forward, spoke: "It is a gift from Pearl. She said I could play with it."

"To understand, you have to imagine what is in the wagon," I said, holding Caroline's hand.

The Vicar searched for an explanation. "Where do I start?"

"You might start by telling us about the Rutledge plantation in Jackson County?" Hatch spoke up.

Surprised, he shook his head in agreement, "You would like to know why a man named Horace Rutledge needs a hundred sixty-two slaves on a thirty-acre plantation."

"I thought it was one hundred and twelve slaves." Hatch said, amending the Vicar's count.

The Vicar nodded his head in agreement.

"Yes, you're right. It has been so long I lost count. The hundred-sixty-two slaves are on a fifty-two-acre plantation in Washington County."

We waited for the Vicar to continue.

"Except for Charity, I have known Pearl longer than anyone. When she came to the church, we sat out under the live oak and had the most delightful conversations. We became good and trusting friends. I thought I might be of some help to the child and serve as her guide, a moral compass to keep her on the straight and narrow.

"Instead, I found the devil, ever patient, at work in my life. Through my conceit, he steered me to follow a path of my own creation. Mine

158

was a path of pride and status. Blinded and drowning in a sea of self-worth, I could not see that this small child lived the life and walked the path of Christ." He added, in tears, "Pearl saved me."

We waited for him to continue.

"I also know Pearl's father. A more sinful and abhorrent man, I have not known. He left her to her own means while he worked. When he collected enough coin, he abandoned her for days at a time while he caroused.

"They traveled from plantation to plantation and town to town, doing odd jobs and hauling freight. When left alone, she sought out the children of the slaves as her companions. It was not long before the slaves on these plantations embraced Pearl. In her, they saw a compassion they had not thought possible. They became her family.

"Pearl stayed behind with the midwives and the children while their parents labored in the fields. She possesses the gift of unconditional love. She showed great empathy toward the children when she witnessed the whipping or the sale of their fathers and mothers." With shaking hands and a quiver in his voice, he forced himself to continue.

"Unlike me, who witnessed and professed God in arrogance, hiding behind the doors of a church, Pearl embraced those I chose not to see."

"She witnessed the whipping of a mother as her child looked on. Pearl threw herself over the woman, trying to stop the beating. She came to me but did not mention the lash she had taken and shed no tears over the flesh torn from her own back. The agony Pearl felt was profound, and her pain was sincere. I was there. I witnessed with my own eyes when this child, this blessed child in anguish, wept tears of blood over the beating of a woman she did not even know." No longer able to speak, he held his face in his hands.

A peace then seemed to come over the Vicar. He reached into his vest pocket, removed a handkerchief, and unfolded it. The cloth carried stains the color of pink rose petals. "I carry this so I can touch and feel her compassion and someday, perhaps, be as worthy of God's grace as Pearl."

He took a deep breath and a sip of coffee.

"Pearl came to me, demanding justice for her friends. With no regard for her own well-being, she laid a brick of gold bullion in my hands. She knew they carried great value, calling them her charms to hide them from her father. Her father lusted after wealth. Pearl felt, if he discovered her charms, she would lose her only family, and he would lose his chance to realize that his greatest wealth was her love.

"We have to buy these people and set them free to be with their children," Pearl told me.

"She doesn't value gold. To her, the jewels are items to be played with. If not for her father, she would have shared them freely.

"Others joined with Pearl in her cause. I am one of Pearl's many disciples. The child sleeping in that room has owned and freed over a thousand slaves.

"I have known you all since you were children, and I know, on the matter of bondage, we are of like mind. With the war coming to a close and freedom at hand, Pearl is going to need something I can't give her. That is why she assembled you."

# Chapter XVII

# Conclusion

Pearl eventually discovered the secret concealed within her name and upon reflection, it was easy for me to see. One day Pearl saw the reflection of her name in a mirror and was elated to find that her middle name, Retsyo, was Oyster spelled backwards. She reported to me that oysters are where pearls came from, and her mother must have considered her a pearl. Years later, I stumbled across what I believed is the real secret to Pearl's name. Her last name, Agnusdei, in the original Latin meant, "Lamb of God." Even in my old age, thinking of Pearl warms my heart and brings a tear of joy to my eyes.

The mind-numbing war ground on. We continued to survive on the fringe. It was harder to distinguish the enemy as the lines of battle, once clearly drawn, became blurred. When I contemplate mankind, I now believe we are our own worst enemy.

The Marr and Smith affair became nothing short of a comedy of errors. Two of our leading citizens, Mr. Thomas Orman and Mr. John Ruan were held hostage by the Union for nearly two months as Union blockaders tried to resolve the disappearance of their agents.

It was three weeks before Governor John Milton received notification of the hostage situation. He was misinformed and told that Marr and Smith were white citizens of Apalachicola.

After the wedding, Hatch traveled up-river to the Confederate stronghold at Ricko's bluff and spoke with the Confederate command. Shortly after, three members of the Rebel Guard found themselves detained and questioned by the Confederate command. The captured Rebel Guards reported that although they were not the ones present at the killing of Stillman Smith, they had received word that Marr and Smith were caught selling salted meat to the Union blockade, captured, held, and shot, trying to escape with arms in hand. The Confederate command summarily hung the three remaining Rebel Guards—not for killing my good friend Stillman. That was not possible because he was black but for other crimes committed against white citizens of Florida during a time of war.

I was angry. They should have hung for killing my friend, but I would have to be satisfied that they were dead.

It all concluded shortly after I received a report from my young agents at the dock late one night. William Marr was seen rowing back to the blockade. The information cost me another pocket full of coins. I never knew the content of Marr's report to the Union and never saw Marr again.

Vicar Horace Rutledge died in February, 1867 at the age of eight-five. "He was a good man," Charity said.

Before he received the calling, he was a young man torn by a forbidden love for a beautiful, black slave. She became pregnant and soon after was sold on the auction block to a merchant named Thomas Orman. Horace moved closer to his forbidden love to help raise and counsel his son.

Charity's oldest son, Reverend Matthew Rutledge paid his respects to the graves of his mother and father in June of 1867. There was a strong family resemblance. With the help of his mother and father, Matthew had purchased his own freedom and ministered to plantation and work camp slaves. He was one of Pearl's many friends.

We were all saddened when Reverend Rutledge reported that after the Battle of Chickamauga his younger brother, John Milton, known as simply, Milton, Charity's baby boy could not accept the role he played in the war. He placed the barrel of a revolver in his mouth and pulled the trigger. We all prayed the exceptional life of his mother would somehow pave his way to salvation.

For a time, Pearl allowed herself to become the child of her dreams. Caroline and I enjoyed our lives as a family, learning from one another. We were blessed with two more children: Anna and Jacob. Pearl shared in our joy and was the best of sisters.

As Pearl had ordained, Uncle Jacob and Aunt Lottie made it official. Lottie's compassion would temper Jacob's steel as she held him through many long nights, shielding him from the nightmares of his past.

Jacob was elected town Marshal. I gave Jacob and Lottie the old home place on Laurel Street as a wedding gift, thanking him for a debt I could never hope to repay.

Caroline and I, with our family, lived in the Cedar Street house I had brought from St. Joseph.

Those who helped Pearl along the way never saw great riches, but she made sure they wanted for nothing. Pearl lived modestly and soon found other causes that required her attentions. Pearl never revealed where she found the treasure.

Over time, we made many trips to Vermont to visit and check on the well-being of our extended family, Stillman's wife and children.

Middlebury College received a generous donation from "'nonymous" donor in 1883 and began admitting women to the college. Stillman's daughters both received a college education, excelling beyond their father's expectations. I made sure they knew their father was a hero, my friend, and he considered them his greatest treasures.

Hatch was Hatch, and thank God, he would always be Hatch. He married a young wildcat from Columbus, Georgia, much to the disapproval of his mother. He was incredibly happy for nearly six months before she left him for a medical doctor and moved west.

He recovered quickly from the experience, and the stories he told of that conquest, although exciting and entertaining, could be repeated only in rooms of men, bourbon, and cigars.

The town's most eligible bachelor, he never suffered for companionship. Rumor had it that you couldn't throw a rock in a crowd without hitting one of his kids. He eventually married a young widow and tried to settle down, but the river called out to him, and he was off again. He didn't leave a grass widow behind. It was to his good fortune that she liked traveling just as much as he did. They had five children and lived on a one-hundred-forty-five-foot sidewheeler, named *Apalachicola Pride*.

Pearl married for love, a good and decent man in June of 1872. Our granddaughter, Olivia, was born in April of the following year. I was happy that Pearl knew the love of a good man and my granddaughter knew family. Tragedy struck in 1880 when he died of consumption, but even this tragedy would serve to strengthen our family bonds.

Time catches up to all of us, I told Pearl. Save enough back to live comfortably in your old age.

"Gold is fleeting. What happens when the box is empty?" I asked.

She smiled an enigmatic smile I had come to recognize so well.

"Don't worry about treasures here on earth Father. Olivia knows where I found it. She can always get the rest."

The End

# References

Willoughby, Lynn. Fair to Middlin': The Antebellum Cotton Trade of the Apalachicola/Chattahoochee River Valley. University of Alabama Press, Tuscaloosa, Alabama. 1993.

Sherlock, Vivian. The Fever Man: A Biography of Dr. John Gorrie. V. M. Sherlock. 1982.

Zinn, Howard. A People's History of the United States: 1492 to Present. Harper Perennial Modern Classics. New York. 2005.

Nichols, Jimmie J. "1836—1986 Sesquicentennial History of Trinity Episcopal Church, Apalachicola, Florida," Jimmie J. Nichols. 1987.

Smith, Julia Floyd. Slavery and Plantation Growth in Antebellum Florida 1821—1860. University Press of Florida. Gainesville, Florida. 1973.

Rogers, William Warren. Outposts on the Gulf: Saint George Island & Apalachicola from Early Exploration to World War II. University of West Florida Press. Pensacola, Florida. 1986

Mueller, Edward A. Perilous Journeys: A History of Steamboating on the Chattahoochee, Apalachicola, and Flint Rivers, 1828 — 1928. Historic Chattahoochee. 1990.

Turner, Maxine. Naval Operations on the Apalachicola and Chattahoochee Rivers 1861 — 1865. Alabama Historical Quarterly. 1975.

Rose, P.K. The Civil War: Black American Contributions to Union intelligence. CIA Center for the Study of Intelligence. U.S. Government. Washington. D.C. 2007.

West, G.M., Old St. Joe, 1922, taken from The Pensacola Gazette, Aug. 7, 1841, Sept. 1844.

Owens, Harry P. "Apalachicola Before 1861." Florida State University, PhD. Dissertation. University Microfilms, Inc., Ann Arbor, Michigan. 1966. (Thank You Harry). Dissertation published in a book of the same name by the Apalachicola Area Historical Society and Patrons of the Apalachicola Library Society. 2014

John Milton to Col. W. J. Magill, Feb. 20, 1864. Milton Letterbook, 44, Florida State Archives, Tallahassee. OR Union and Confederate Navies in the War of the Rebellion, Series I, Vol. 17, 350.

# Photo Credits

Orman family archives. Photos, Orman House, Sadie Orman

Credit for the following photos to the State Archives of Florida "Florida Memory Project:

Steamboat loaded with cotton, PR00373
Dragging Florida Down, By: Matt Morgan Image RC08563
Cape Saint George Lighthouse. Image RC03152
Chase of the Blockade Runner. Image RC05589
Workers gathering sap from turpentine pines. Image RC01685
Turpentine still. Image PR12612

Stars and Bars Flag: File: Confederate 'Stars and Bars' Flag, captured at Columbia, South Carolina-Wisconsin Veterans Museum-
DSC02996.JPG

Apalachicola Pearl | Michael Kinnett

# About the Author

After a working career and raising two daughters, my wife and I moved to the Florida Panhandle. It was in the historic town of Apalachicola that I began creating and caring for the Orman House State Park Museum. When I started the house was an empty shell. Immersed in local history, I now enjoy sharing Apalachicola's rich heritage with thousands of visitors from around the world. Apalachicola Pearl was born from my passion for the town's history and its people. My sincere wish is for you to enjoy reading Apalachicola Pearl as much as I enjoyed writing her.

Apalachicola Pearl | Michael Kinnett

CPSIA information can be obtained
at www.ICGtesting.com
Printed in the USA
LVHW110812080720
660056LV00002B/222